Death of a Bear

A Provincetown Mystery

Jeannette de Beauvoir

Death of a Bear: A Provincetown Mystery
Copyright © 2017 by Jeannette de Beauvoir
Published by HomePort Press
PO Box 1508
Provincetown, MA 02657
www.HomePortPress.com

ISBN   978-0-9974327-9-4
eISBN 978-0-9974327-8-7
Cover Design by Victoria Landis

Death of a Bear is a work of fiction. Names, characters, places, situations, and incidents are the products of the author's imagination and used fictitiously. Any resemblance to actual events, locales, or persons, living or dead, is purely coincidental.

Other Books
by Jeannette de Beauvoir

Mysteries:
In Dark Woods
The Martine LeDuc series:
    Deadly Jewels
    Asylum
The Trinity Pierce series:
    Murder Most Academic (as Alicia Stone)

Historical Fiction:
Our Lady of the Dunes
The Crown & The Kingdom

1

There isn't much you can't do in Provincetown.

Not in the summer, anyway. Fewer than one thousand people live in my town at the tip of Cape Cod from October through the end of March. During the summer, that population goes up to 30,000. The same streets that echoed plaintively—and coldly—in the winter months are overrun with people...and I mean *people*. Commercial Street, our main drag, is supposedly for use by vehicles, but you try driving from one end of it to the other in August. Just try. I *dare* you.

I'm supposed to like the tourists. We're all supposed to like the tourists. They're our livelihood, every last one of us year-rounders, in one way or another. And sometimes, truth be told, I really do like them. I am, after all, pretty lucky: I get to be with certain visitors on the best day of their lives. I'm the wedding coordinator for the Race Point Inn, one of Provincetown's most prestigious hostelries—with a price tag to match—and this town is Destination Wedding Central, especially for the gay population. Which is, truth be told, most of our population. Massachusetts led the way in marriage equality, and we're still pretty fiercely proud of that fact.

I do a *lot* of weddings.

I wasn't thinking of weddings that Friday. I was thinking that I must be suicidal to try and do any grocery shopping at the town's only supermarket at the very beginning of Bear Week. Like I said, there's not much you can't do in Provincetown, but buying milk, bread, and cat food on the weekend is definitely out of the running. I was on my bicycle (I'm not so suicidal as to actually take my car anywhere) and having problems finding a place on the bike rack outside the Stop and Shop when someone tapped me on the shoulder. "Sydney, princess! I was hoping I'd run into you!"

I knew who it was before I even turned around; the voice is famous. Vernon Porter is something of a celebrity around P'town. As himself, he's one of the town's listed wedding officiants, so I get to work with him quite a lot. As his alter ego, Lady Di (think middle-aged overweight cross-dresser with big hair), he's a radio personality with a kick-ass oldies show on community radio on Friday nights. "Hey, Vernon."

He enveloped me in a fierce hug and a cloud of perfume. I think my grandmother smelled like that. "Sydney, darling, do you have any weddings for me? I was supposed to marry that couple from Connecticut, but they eloped on me, those bad boys."

"Nothing at the moment," I said. "I'll let you know if anything last-minute comes up." We usually arrange weddings at least six months in advance, but there's always some-one impetuous with a last-minute decision, and Vernon's always ready to oblige.

I'd gotten my bicycle more or less in place. "Why are you here, anyway?" I asked. "Shouldn't you be getting ready for your show?"

"Just picking up a few necessities," he said, his voice squeaking on the word "necessities" so I'd think it was something naughty.

"Seriously," I said, "I don't want to know. I'm too young and innocent."

He gave a hoot of laughter and enveloped me again in his arms and ancient perfume. "Remember, if anything comes up, give me a call. All my couples love me."

"I know, Vernon."

"They send me pictures. They take me to dinner."

"I know, Vernon."

"All right. Kiss-kiss."

Shopping at the supermarket is never a straightforward endeavor in Provincetown. In the winter, you make your way slowly from aisle to aisle, at every turn seeing someone you know and haven't talked to in a while. Stop & Shop as Information Central. In the summer, making your way *anywhere* in the supermarket is a trial by patience, as chances are good that you're going to get stuck at least three times behind groups of tourists stocking up for cookouts and brunches. And tourists, as we all know, have a blind spot. Probably several. Not just in the aisles, either; they come and spend amazing amounts of money that keep the town afloat… but that we can't help but envy.

Most of us who live here year-round aren't particularly wealthy. Some of us were born here and are grittily determined to stay, no matter how much gentrification comes our way. The rest of us are called "washashores" and mainly came here because we felt, for one reason or another, that we had to. Artists and writers who got fellowships to the Fine Arts Work Center and found their muse; gay men who came here during the scourge of the '80s and then didn't die after all; tourists who fell in love with the place and spent the next five years figuring a way to live here. There's a soup kitchen in the winter. There's interminable talk about the dearth of affordable housing. In the summer, people work three, four, five jobs; in the winter there's one job if they're lucky, unemployment if they're not.

And then the summer—"the season"—comes and the rich flood into town, eating fifteen-dollar hamburgers and renting $10,000-a-week condos and getting drunk and silly in the streets.

It's my time, the season. I spend most of the winter planning weddings, and the spring, summer, and fall making sure that everything connected to them goes smoothly. Or as close to smoothly as I can approximate, given Murphy's Law, whether or not Venus is in retrograde, and the sheer ornery nature of life. In March I love it. By October I'm ready to shoot somebody, preferably myself.

For all of this I make enough money to get by, pay the rent on my miniscule apartment, and keep my cat, Ibsen, in the style to which he's become accustomed. Now, if I were a *real* P'townie, I'd have a dog, but I have neither the patience nor the fortitude to live with a creature that demands such a high level of commitment and attention. I'm not married anymore, for the same reason. I will say that I admire those who *can* put up with either a dog, a spouse or, in some cases, both.

I headed in to the store to pick up cat food, oranges, bread, and assorted vegetables. I too had someone waiting for me at home. The human food could be skipped; the cat food could not. And a salad would be good.

"Happy Bear Week, Sydney!" I nodded and raised my hand; I was at the salad bar and determined to get through in less than twenty minutes. The middle-aged woman next to me, wearing shorts and flip-flops and a t-shirt that read, *I shucked oysters in Wellfleet,* looked around. "Bear Week?" she asked.

So much for the twenty minutes, but we all need to be nice to them. I smiled brightly. "It's one of Provincetown's annual theme weeks," I said. Sydney Riley, Answers While You Wait, that's me. "We have all these different festivals that celebrate groups of people— like families, for example, or women."

She frowned. "*Bears?*"

"Bears," I said carefully, "are gay men who are large and have beards and are particularly– um–hairy. They're generally attracted to other men who are also large and bearded."

I think she might have been wishing she hadn't asked. She was looking at the plastic container in her hands as though wondering how it had gotten there. I had a sudden impulse to assure her that, unlike the ones in the wild, *our* bears weren't likely to attack. "People come from all over the world for it," I said instead. "It really is a Thing."

Most people who come to P'town know that it's a significantly gay destination, but there is still the odd vacationer who gets taken by surprise. Some tour company brings busloads of people from Baptist churches here in the fall; *someone* had a twisted sense of humor. I wondered what Salad Bar Lady was going to tell her family.

Lucky she wasn't here for Circuit-Boy week, I thought. Bears are lovely. Their larger body types contain some of the kindest hearts in the world. If a bear were to accidentally step on you, he would be the first to apologize and feel awful for potentially hurting you. Not every week is this pleasant.

So you can see already that as far as premonitions go, I am completely lame. This week, as it turned out, was going to be anything but pleasant.

I managed to get through checkout and to my bicycle with a minimum of trouble. My apartment is above a dance club, which makes for almost-but-not-quite-affordable rent and free Lady Gaga at one-thirty in the morning when I'm trying to sleep. I put the groceries in the refrigerator, gave Ibsen a treat or three, and checked my email.

That was when the day blew up.

It was a note from the couple getting married the next day. The next *day*. "Dear Ms. Riley, sorry to spring this on you, but we decided to invite Marcel's family after all, at the last minute. It'll mean so much to them. So that's only an extra sixteen people. That's fine, right? You're the best! See you tomorrow!"

Sixteen people. Sixteen *more* people. I felt the panic I always get whenever anything unexpected happens—which, in the wedding business, is pretty much all the time. What can I do now about 16 extra people? There's no space in the dining room. I don't have enough chairs for the ceremony. What about food? What about…?

Stop, I told myself fiercely. *Breathe. Just breathe. You'll be okay. It'll be okay. We'll make it work.*

Ibsen was looking at me quizzically. "I'll be back," I promised him. *Breathe, Riley, just breathe.* Ibsen didn't care. He turned away, his tail twitching with disdain.

Downstairs, I unchained my bicycle—P'town enjoys relatively low crime overall, but for some reason we have the most bicycle thefts per capita in the nation—and headed over to the inn, reminding myself to breathe as I pedaled. The panic was subsiding slightly. *Barry will help figure it out.*

Jason was at the inn's front desk. His willowy figure was attired, today, in a sharp Hawaiian shirt. Wrong continent, but what the hell. "*Hello*, beautiful lady," he said brightly. "I just *have* to tell you about this horrible couple that called for you earlier—you wouldn't believe what some people want—"

"No time," I interrupted. "Where's Barry?"

Jason looked affronted. "Don't you want to hear…?"

I usually like Jason. Usually. I glared at him and he relented. "Over at the pool bar, darling," he said with resignation. "But do come by and see me before you leave. I'm so tragically lonely here."

"Tragic, maybe." I couldn't help myself. I do like Jason. I headed out through the breakfast room to the outdoor pool with its bar.

Race Point is really a beautiful inn, managing to keep the quaint feel that people love in P'town while still offering all the amenities that they really want. It's like a town within a town, with a spa, three dining areas, a sitting room, a swimming pool complete with hot tub, an outdoor events area, and—of course—three bars. There's a fair amount of drinking that takes place here in the season. And out of it, too.

Barry was standing behind the bar frowning at a receipt. "It's still not adding up," he said to the bartender, someone new I didn't know, who was looking suitably abashed.

If Barry was unhappy about something as small as a receipt, he was going to have a heart attack over *my* news. Great. "Hey, Barry," I said, sliding onto one of the empty barstools. "What is it, Hawaiian Day? First Jason and now you."

"We're doing a luau party tonight," Barry said absently. He and Jason might have bought their shirts at the same place, but in very different departments. Where Jason was willowy and elegant, Barry was solid, with a baby bump that had nothing to do with babies. Dark curly hair and beard, hairy arms.

In short, this was one of Barry's favorite weeks in Provincetown, because Barry was a bear.

"I have a problem," I told him. The bartender smiled at me.

"We all have problems," Barry agreed, looking at the receipt.

"My name's Gus," the bartender told me. "Nice to meet you."

I frowned at him. Men don't often come on to women in Provincetown. Not at the Race Point Inn, anyway. The bartender smiled again.

I tore my gaze away and looked back at Barry. "I have a wedding tomorrow," I said.

"I know, pumpkin. What was it, Gus, a Cosmo?"

"They've just added sixteen people," I said conversationally. Just sitting near Barry was calming. Bears tend to have that effect on me. They're generally the nicest people in town. My boss is the nicest bear during a week filled with nice bears.

He glanced up at me and cracked a smile. His eyes were twinkling. "You-know-who's not going to like that," he said.

So he *was* listening. I speared an olive from the garnish tray and ate it. Gus was still looking at me. I wondered if my mascara was running or something like that. "Uh-huh," I said.

He shrugged. "I'll deal with her," he said. "And you'll need more chairs for the ceremony."

"I can get them," I said. Or at least I hoped I could. "That's it, then? You're not nervous about her reaction?"

"Why would I be? She works for me, doesn't she?"

Adrienne, the executive chef at Race Point was brilliant, creative, and a diva. Better he should be the one to tell her; as he pointed out, she did work for him. "Okay," I said and took another olive.

"Would you like a drink?" asked Gus.

"No, I wouldn't," I said. "No, she wouldn't," said Barry at the same time.

Gus looked like we'd ruined his day. I peered at him a little more closely. Was it really possible that Barry had hired someone *straight?* "Okay," I said again. "Sixteen more people. I'll get the chairs, you'll square it with Adrienne. Oh, and Martin." Martin is the maître d' in our main restaurant, and supervises events at the inn involving food. That includes wedding receptions, which put us frequently in somewhat adversarial roles. He was going to have to figure out where to fit all these extra people.

"He works for me, too," said Barry. He caught my glance. "What? Sydney, my love, you bring more business to this place than the two of them combined. I have my priorities. *You* get whatever you want." He paused. "Within reason."

I leaned across the bar and kissed his cheek. "Within reason," I agreed. "I love you, Barry."

"Of course you do," he said. "Get out of here. You have chairs to order."

I got out of there, wending my way around oiled bodies in skimpy suits soaking up the late-afternoon sun. The panic was gone. Maybe I'd go have a drink, after all.

Just not at the poolside bar at the Race Point Inn.

2

The first Saturday of Bear Week.

I pulled on jeans and a t-shirt, brushed my teeth, ran a brush through my often-tangled brown hair and some makeup over my eyes and that that was it for toiletries. I had work to do.

Two bears—hefty men with beards—were checking in as I passed the front desk and Jason interrupted their conversation with a muttered apology. "Sydney? There was someone looking for you."

"Did it have to do with today?" Not another sixteen people, surely. Nobody has that many people who want to come to their wedding at the last minute.

"I don't think so. A nice-looking man." In Jason-speak, that meant a good body. "Said he'd be back." He rolled his eyes at the bears, including them in the conversation. "She gets *all* the good ones!" They chuckled good-naturedly and I made a face at him over their shoulders.

I passed through the swimming-pool area, already beginning to fill up with sun-seekers, and out to the outdoor patio where we do weddings. It looks like everything you wanted your wedding backdrop to be: a bower, enough plants to give some privacy (at a premium in this town, believe me), slate underfoot, a Zen garden with a fountain in a corner.

The florists were already there, working on the bower, and as they seemed to know what they were doing I didn't interrupt. Instead I pulled out my iPhone and called Barry. "Did you square things with Martin and Adrienne?"

"And good morning to you," he grunted. He sounded like he'd been asleep. Well, he'd probably been up late with his Hawaiian thing last night. "What is it?"

"Martin. Adrienne. Sixteen extra people for the wedding. Are we good?"

"Of course we're good." Another grunt. "What time is it?"

"Nearly ten."

"God, Sydney!" I took that to mean I'd interrupted his hibernation too early. "I'll be down in an hour."

Barry lived at the inn. In fact, I was reasonably sure that if he could swing it, Barry would never leave the inn. He loved it like a child. He'd bought it back when real people could actually buy real estate in this town, and had built it up with a solid reputation for charm and elegance. And good food.

And weddings.

I pulled out my planner and started down the list. Florists on the spot. Champagne for the wedding toast being delivered at eleven. String quartet already on their way from up-Cape. Adrienne and Martin supposedly dealing with whatever problems an extra sixteen people presented. The additional chairs on their way. I didn't worry about the photographer; in the three years we'd worked together, he'd never been late once.

Time, I decided, for another coffee. Brunch was going full swing in the breakfast room, and I skirted the buffet table to go straight for the coffee station. Priorities.

I was filling my cup from the imposing samovar when a man came in from the reception area and headed straight toward me. "Ms. Riley? The front desk told me where you were."

I was going to have to have a word with the front desk. I don't like anything that comes between me and my coffee. And I knew right away that there was a problem here: the only time a man wears a suit in Provincetown is if he's getting married or buried, and sometimes not even then. It was a light gray suit and looked wildly out of place among the shorts and t-shirts and flip-flops. A nice suit, granted, but a suit nonetheless. About my age, a few inches taller than me, with hair that was just starting its journey toward gray and dark eyes with ridiculously long lashes that made them seem darker.

Oh, God, I thought: a lawyer. He had to be a lawyer. I was getting sued. Somebody somewhere hadn't liked something about their wedding and was suing me. I cleared my throat and fought down the panic. *Breathe. Breathe through it.* "I'm Sydney Riley."

He reached into an inner pocket and produced, not the subpoena I was dreading (I do manage to go from zero to panic in mere seconds), but a badge wallet. "Agent Ali Hakim.

US Immigrations and Customs Enforcement."

I don't know what Miss Manners would have counseled as an appropriate response. Probably not mine. "*You're* Immigration?" I squeaked.

A smile, very white teeth. "One of the token Arabs," he acknowledged. He probably had to acknowledge it eighteen times a day. "My parents are Lebanese."

"Sorry," I said. "Stupid thing to say." I made a face. "Racist, too."

"Not uncommon," he said. "Can we sit down for a moment?"

"As long as I can bring my coffee. Do you want some?"

He shook his head. "No, thanks." He'd probably hate our coffee; he probably drank something strong and electric and Turkish. Or was that a racist thought, too? It was all so complicated.

We sat on a loveseat in one of the groupings off the reception area and I put my cup on the low table in front of us. Beyond my shallow surface thoughts about who he was, I was starting to feel something cold stirring in my stomach. Like a lot of people I know, I'm not exactly thrilled with the direction the US is taking regarding immigration restrictions, and in my book, ICE are definitely the Bad Guys.

He wasn't in a hurry. He sat down, a fluid, elegant movement. He looked around himself (probably checking to see if any undocumented people were lurking in the room's periphery). He gestured toward my cup. "Did you know that coffee is the second-most traded commodity on earth?" he asked easily. "Oil is number one, of course, but twenty-five million farmers grow coffee."

When I'm nervous, I get sarcastic. "What is that supposed to be?" I asked. "Government small talk?"

He looked, if anything, amused. "Just trying to be polite. It's not you I'm interested in, Ms. Riley."

"You sure know your way to a girl's heart." I took a swallow of coffee.

"Officially speaking, of course." The guy was smooth. "But I do have some interest in Mr. Parker."

"Barry?" I stared at him. "Barry's as American as apple pie." And had ingested more than his share of said pies. "He was born in upstate New York. Schenectady, I think." We'd gotten drunk together one night, me and Barry, and exchanged life stories. Okay, more than just *one* night. "You don't get much more American than Barry."

He sighed, sat back more in the sofa, crossed his legs. "He's a citizen, all right. So are you. So is everybody currently working at the Race Point Inn."

"You checked us all out? What is this, my tax dollars at work?" It wasn't altogether surprising, though: along with the influx of tourists during the season, we have an influx of workers to tend to them. A lot of Jamaicans and Eastern Europeans, some South Americans. I was pretty sure there were establishments in town that weren't as squeaky-clean as us, places that paid people under the table, didn't check work permits.

"You do a lot of weddings, here at the inn," he said.

"Yes," I said slowly. I still couldn't see where this was going.

He pulled out a small notebook from his inner jacket pocket and consulted it. "More, in fact, than anyplace else in Provincetown."

"We have better facilities than anyplace else in Provincetown."

"Fifty-four last summer. Twelve in October. Eight in *January*." He looked up from the notebook. "Tell me, Ms. Riley, is there really a rush on weddings in a resort town in the dead of January?"

"We're one of the most popular destinations for same-sex weddings in the country," I said primly, reciting by rote. The words were automatic; my mind was racing. *Breathe, Riley.* "Massachusetts was the first state to legalize marriage equality."

"What is this supposed to be?" he asked with the ghost of a smile. "Wedding-coordinator small talk?"

"Touché." But I still couldn't see where this was going.

"And a lot of your couples aren't from the States," he said. "Or, at any rate, one-*half* of a lot of your couples aren't from here."

"Words that sound strange coming from *you*, Agent Hakim," I said. Where was he going with this? Yeah, of course, we *do* get a lot of non-USian people getting married, but it's a time-honored practice, finding the path to citizenship through love and marriage. I couldn't see anything wrong with it.

He lifted an eyebrow and answered my unspoken question. "I was born in Boston. And you can call me Ali if that's more comfortable."

"Nothing about this conversation is comfortable." I made a show of gulping some coffee—now getting cold—and putting the cup back down with finality. "And I don't think I can help, no matter what I call you. We do weddings. We do a lot of weddings. If you ever decide to tie the knot, come see us."

Damn, did I just show that I'd checked out his ring finger? "But that doesn't mean we're operating the matrimonial equivalent of a puppy mill here." I was just warming up. "News flash to the current administration: People fall in love when they're traveling. Sometimes they even bring their new partner home and marry them. There's nothing nefarious about that." I stood up. "And as I have a wedding today at noon"—I consulted my watch—"in exactly an hour and a half, I hope that you'll excuse me."

He stood up, effortless. Jason would have checked out his muscles on the way. I tried not to. "I know that Mr. Parker is very popular," he said. "I know that nobody wants to think ill of him. And I'm sorry to be the messenger here. But you need to know that this investigation has to run its course. It isn't going away."

"Then you'll have to do it without me," I snapped. "Seriously. *This* is how you spend your time? Do you think that any of the people we marry are terrorists? Because I can assure you—"

"It's not about terrorism, Ms. Riley. It's about the law. It's illegal to sell green cards."

I stopped in mid-flounce. "Selling green cards? Is *that* what you think we're doing?"

He smiled. "Have a nice day, Ms. Riley."

Just like the Feds, I thought. Always have to have the last word.

3

The wedding came off with a minimum of glitches, despite my misgivings, with Adrienne and Martin giving me only a few dirty looks. By the time it was over the ICE agent had blessedly disappeared. I didn't know if he'd spoken to Barry or not, and when I saw my boss later in the afternoon he didn't bring it up, and so I didn't, either.

Jason was all a-twitter, though. "Did you see that *suit*?"

I nodded. I was consulting the wedding calendar behind the reception desk. "Couldn't miss it. Stood out like a…" I floundered and looked over at him. "Help me. What's the analogy I want?"

Jason wasn't interested in pursuing linguistic topics. "A dreamboat," he said, and sighed. "Tall, dark, and handsome."

"You think in clichés," I told him.

"They only get to be clichés because they're true," he countered. "Give me one night, I could show him how the other half lives."

"What does that mean?"

"Oh, honey," he said, pityingly. "Straight, straight, straight. *All* the good ones are."

I stared at him. First Gus the bartender, and now Ali Hakim. The straight male population of Provincetown had just doubled. Okay, I exaggerate, but still... "I didn't notice," I said.

"You'll stay single forever if you don't *start* noticing," said Jason.

"Who says I don't want to stay single? Are you channeling my mother, or something? Besides, I'm not single. I have Ibsen."

"A cat doesn't count."

"Don't tell him that." I went back to the calendar. "Did the guys from Montpelier check in? I have them on for Tuesday sunset, and then a bonfire at Herring Cove."

"Yes, they're here, in all their ursine finery," Jason said. He's always miffed when I don't take his relationship advice. Which is pretty much all the time.

"Good." And I had a break: no weddings tonight or tomorrow. A very small intimate ceremony on Monday, and then two weddings on Tuesday. The bears doing their official mating during their special week. Looked like I was going to be able to catch up on paperwork, at least.

As long as Immigration stayed out of my way. I allowed myself a moment to think about it. Yeah, we did have a lot of foreigners marrying Americans, but I never saw that as problematic. Love is love, and the fact that there was finally marriage equality was cause for celebration, not a license to start inspecting people's motives. "Jason," I said suddenly.

"Yes, honey?"

"You don't know anything about—" I bit my lip. No; it wasn't worth thinking about. Barry was honest. Barry was one of my two closest friends in the world. There was no way—no *way*—that he'd do anything illegal. And I was still not clear what the illegality was that he was being accused of, anyway. "Never mind," I said.

"Whatevers."

"Okay. My work here is done." I turned away from the calendar and grabbed my keys—even at Race Point Inn, I lock my bike.

"I'm going to the bank and the post office. Might be back later."

"Whatevers." He was looking at his smartphone. Probably on some dating site, though Jason's idea of an ideal date would have me terrified even if I understood what it entailed.

"I'm going now," I said, and managed to get out before the third of his "whatevers." Wobbling along on my bicycle, I plunged bravely into Commercial Street traffic. When I say "traffic," mind you, I'm not talking about vehicles; I'm talking about people. There is one—and at certain points two—perfectly good sidewalks on Commercial Street, but it's a see-and-be-seen kind of place, and everyone just moseys along wherever they want, including (or especially) down the middle of the street. Families with toddlers in strollers or little kids dangerously darting around; groups of friends walking four or five abreast, people stopping short in the middle of the street for a chat, guys just off the ferry wheeling suitcases. Add to that bicycles, pedicabs, and skateboards, and you have chaos. It's actually a lot of fun if you have nowhere that you need to be. It's unavoidable if you need the post office or Seamen's Bank, both of which were on my to-do list.

Color and noise and laughter. Restaurants spilling tables and umbrellas onto the sidewalk; catcalls; music pouring out of art galleries; a drag performer handing out postcards for her show later that night. A dog wheeled in a Radio Flyer wagon behind its two daddies. Women still wearing Hillary Clinton t-shirts. As much as I despair, sometimes, of this town, the truth is that I love it. Every silly inconvenient moment of it.

I stopped in the West End at the bakery-café that's in many ways Bear Central, owned by Lucas (who makes cupcakes to die for) with the occasional assistance of his real-estate broker partner Henry. The place was crowded, as it was all season, though today with more bears than usual. I waited and watched as the guy in front of me bought a couple of oversized bear paw-print t-shirts and a bag of cookies to go with it. "Hey, Lucas."

"Sydney! What brings you down here?" Lucas sometimes does our wedding cakes for special bears—or when Adrienne is having a meltdown.

"I've exercised enough to have earned something sweet," I said. I didn't know if it was true, but I'm easily convinced when sugar is involved.

Lucas grinned and popped some butterscotch haystacks in a bag. "Things going well at the inn?"

"It's Bear Week; what do you think? Busy, busy, busy." I paid him. "How's Henry?"

"He's good. On the phone all the time. I couldn't do it."

"Say hi for me." I didn't want to take up any more of his time; there were hungry bears in line behind me.

"You got it. Be good, Sydney."

Not much chance of anything else, I thought. I was too busy to get into any trouble.

When I got home, Ibsen was waiting for me, reproach in his every sinew. He had been hungry for some time, if I was interpreting his strident vocalization correctly. "So am I, kiddo," I said. I got him something disgusting out of a can and myself something slightly more appetizing out of the freezer, and we settled down companionably to watch a movie. Saturday night at my house. It doesn't get any better than this.

"And ice cream for dessert," I said aloud.

4

I was up early the next morning. Sunday mornings in the summer tend to be lazy affairs, starting slowly with hangovers and progressing to Bloody Marys and chic brunches and maybe a trip to the pool or the beach if you're feeling really energetic.

Not me. For me, Sunday mornings start early, because I have a coveted key to the Race Point Inn's gated swimming pool area, which only officially opens at nine o'clock. If I'm there by 7:30, I can get a good workout in before anybody has even considers getting out of bed. One of the best perks of my job, I've always thought.

I threw a shirt and shorts on over my swimsuit, grabbed my bike, and was unlocking the gate by 7:20. Towels thanks to the inn's spa—another perk—and I was just unbuttoning my shirt when I finally really looked at the water.

And saw that it wasn't empty.

He was floating almost in the very center of the pool, face down, and bobbing gently as the intake ruffled the water in little eddies. Other than that, he wasn't moving. He was fully dressed in a t-shirt and shorts, and it was clear to me—I don't know how, exactly—that he had been there for a while.

In the movies, women who come upon dead bodies tend to scream. My first response was that I was going to be sick. As soon as the nausea subsided, my second response was that I was going to have to see if I could do anything about it. I didn't think there was anything anyone could do at this point, and I very nearly talked myself out of it.

I took a deep breath and eased into the pool at the shallow end. Ew, ew, ew. Waded out to the floating body, which I was pretty sure already was a corpse, but I wouldn't be able to live with myself if I didn't at least *check*...

The swaying water pushed him up against me. Ew, again. I put out a tentative hand, touching his throat and feeling for a pulse. The water was cold. The body was cold. There was no sign of life.

I knew who it was, of course. Even if his girth hadn't given him away—and during Bear Week it would be understandable if it hadn't—I would still have recognized Barry Parker. My friend and erstwhile boss, now reduced to a body in the pool. And ironically enough, he didn't even swim.

Which could be why he'd drowned. Slipped and hit his head and fallen in? But why would he have been out here alone? There had been some sort of bear party last night; he shouldn't have been alone. And if he wasn't alone, why hadn't anyone jumped in to help him? *Breathe. Breathe.* Unlike Barry, who couldn't.

I was thinking all this as I was laboriously water-walking back to the steps at the shallow end of the pool. I hadn't brought my phone with me, and I ran through the courtyard to reception, my hands shaking, my teeth chattering. I dropped the keys twice while I was trying to unlock the door. I swore under my breath and finally got it to work. I flung the door open and ran to the phone—I have no idea why I thought that speed was essential, Barry certainly wasn't going anywhere—and punched 911.

I didn't even realize that I was crying until after they told me they were coming.

***

Two hours later I hadn't gone anywhere.

It's a long and tedious process, apparently, that gets set into motion when somebody dies. On television the detectives just ask a few questions, peek at the body, quickly identify a potential suspect if there's foul play, and the plot moves on.

In real life, though, there's an awful lot of hurry-up-and-wait.

I was busily comparing the real thing with the TV version because it kept my mind away from Barry, the real person, my friend and boss, a man I cared deeply about. The moment I'd touched him in the pool I'd known that he was gone, that something irreparable had happened, something beautiful and irreplaceable had shattered.

It was the beginning of July, and I was freezing.

I'd called Mike Pearson, the inn's manager, and woken him up. He wasn't pleased. "What do you mean, Barry's dead?"

"I mean Barry's dead," I said, "and any minute now some guest is going to come down and—"

"I'm on my way," he said. He arrived just after the paramedics from the fire department, and kindly brought me a fluffy robe from the spa to put around me, as it was clear I wasn't going anywhere for a while. Mike might be a lot less personable than our boss, but he's much more businesslike, and he was already assessing what this was going to mean for the inn's commerce. "We can just lock off the pool area," he said.

"Won't the police do that?"

"I have no idea what the police will do," he said. He sounded cranky. He'd probably had other plans for the day. He went back to the kitchen to talk to the breakfast cooks and wait staff; I had no idea what he was telling them, but no one appeared in reception to see what was going on.

I sat on a bar stool in my fluffy robe, my hands wrapped around a cup of coffee that Jason had thoughtfully delivered, looking at the pool and wondering what the hell had happened there. Mike had been my first call; Jason was his. And rightly so. Jason was slick and smooth, taking over the reception area, steering guests away from the iron gate leading to the pool, murmuring something about an accident and ushering them into the dining room for breakfast.

An accident. How on earth had Barry fallen into the pool? *When* had Barry fallen into the pool? Barry is—was—a hearty drinker for sure, and I'd definitely seen him well over capacity more than a few times, but surely whoever served him had also kept an eye on him? Unless he had come down from his own suite during the night and fallen in the pool in the dark…but why would he have even *been* in that area? It's locked at night; liability and all that. Much more likely that he'd have come down and helped himself to one of our two indoor bars, not the outside one in the euphemistically called fitness area. It didn't make sense.

And then they hauled Barry out of the pool and I saw his face.

5

There are some things that, once you've seen them, you can't unsee. Camping with my family, I once accidentally caught a glimpse of my father naked, and will never *ever* get that unfortunate picture out of my mind. When I was in college I drove by a car crash on a highway when they were still pulling the bodies out, and it still haunts my sleep sometimes, that image.

And now Barry's face. It didn't look like Barry. It didn't even look *human*.

"What happened to him?" I gasped, and one of the uniformed officers—Celia Towers, it was, we know all the cops in town—gave me a quick look. "Don't watch," she said, not without sympathy.

"I have to," I said, not even understanding what I meant. It was as though abandoning him right now, leaving him alone to these impersonal hands and this professional inquiry, was somehow unthinkable. "What made him look like that?"

She touched my arm, lightly. "Why don't you go get yourself some more coffee?" she suggested. "There are people who will want to talk to you, but you don't have to wait right here."

"Coffee's in the dining room," I said. "I don't think I can face guests yet. And I don't want to leave Barry." Even to my own ears, I sounded stubborn and petulant.

Celia shook her head. "Just don't look, then," she said. "Really, Sydney. Believe me. You don't want to watch."

But of course I already had, my stomach signaling that I was again dangerously close to throwing up, and I fell back on my mantra. *Breathe. Breathe through it. Just breathe.* After a couple of deep breaths, I steadied myself and looked again. But they'd already covered him with a sheet—one thing an inn can provide in bulk is bed linens—and I figured that was just as well. His expression had already burned its way into my brain.

I couldn't imagine getting drunk, falling into a pool, and drowning. Well, I *could* imagine it, but nothing I could imagine would put that expression on anyone's face. Drowning, I'd read somewhere, was one of the better ways to die. Gentle.

Barry, my gentle bear, had not died gently. Barry had died in pain. Intense pain.

What the *hell* had happened?

***

No one told me, of course.

They came and interviewed me right there, at the bar. I'd already told everything I knew to the EMTs and the first uniformed police who arrived, but they wanted me to stick around and say it all over again to the detectives. About finding Barry. About Barry in general. I was tiring fast and had this horrible feeling creeping from my gut into my chest. It was finally sinking in that Barry was *gone*.

And that I was going to miss him more than I could begin to imagine. Barry was part of my world, of my days, of my life. Barry had always been there, from the first moment we'd met. We'd had our ups and downs, of course, but we'd stayed friends somehow through them all.

Barry was gone.

Julie Agassi was there by then. She's the head of Provincetown's detective bureau and another friend; and I badly needed a friend. The two uniformed cops had already put tape up around the pool area and Julie looked at Barry under his sheet for a long time before coming over to me. "Sorry, Sydney."

My teeth were still chattering. "He's dead," I said, pointing out the obvious.

Julie nodded and hugged me briefly, a sort of side hug, shoulder to shoulder, reassuring. "I know," she said. "I'm sorry. I promise, I'll do the best I can for him."

I nodded, but that actually meant a lot. Julie had once told me that if you want to commit a crime, the best place to do it is on the Cape. We don't have the most organized law enforcement in the world—understatement of the year there—and levels of competence vary wildly between, and within, each police department. I swallowed bile. "What *happened*, Julie?"

"I don't know," she said, her gaze traveling around, looking casual but seeing everything. "Right now I'm just calling it an unattended death. But I'm pulling in the state crime lab, just in case." She grimaced. "Have to light something under them. Once this place gets going, there won't be any point in looking for evidence." She squeezed my arm.

"Stick around, Sydney. I'll get you out of here as quickly as I can."

So I watched, numb, as more people arrived. Crime-scene techs from the state police came and took samples of everything from pool water to something that looked suspiciously like vomit. A photographer documented everything.

I just got colder and colder.

Jason came and kept me company for a while, perching on the barstool next to mine and sharing mad speculations about what might have happened. "Did he have a secret lover, do you suppose, Sydney? I mean, besides Glenn?"

I shook my head. "I can't imagine it," I said. Glenn was Barry's longtime partner. He lived in Key West, ran a bar there, came to Provincetown for a few weeks in the summer. He was due to arrive… "Oh, God," I said, remembering. "Glenn's coming today." I turned to look at him in horror. "Jason, Glenn's coming *today*!"

"Mike will deal with it," Jason said, uninterested. He and Glenn didn't get along. "Maybe someone broke in, was robbing the inn, and Barry found them. They could have stayed after the party last night. They could've hidden somewhere, and that's when Barry caught 'em."

That was a thought. I frowned. "You opened the front desk," I said. "Was anything missing?"

"Mike opened the front desk," he said absently. He was working on another scenario. "But it's a good bet, isn't it? People would assume this place has money somewhere, especially if they're tweakers. Or maybe Barry went to the A-House and picked somebody up, and they robbed him and pushed him in the pool."

The A-House is the Atlantic House, one of the oldest clubs in town. Tennessee Williams frequented the Little Bar, and it's said that it's where he wrote *The Glass Menagerie*, sitting right there at the bar. The club on the upper floor is famous for excruciatingly loud music and a vibrant predominantly male pick-up scene.

"I don't know," I said doubtfully.

Jason was enjoying his theory. "A new bear in town," he suggested. "Just what he needed before Glenn got here and he had to be monogamous."

"Stop it," I said sharply. I liked Glenn. I'd loved Barry. And Jason was sounding like a gossip columnist. "Stop being mean. It's shallow and it's horrible and it's not like you at all, and I hope to high heaven this wasn't what you're saying, because then Glenn will have to think about that for the rest of his life."

Jason was unaffected by Glenn's possible future thoughts. "Well, he didn't fall into the pool by himself, did he?" he asked rhetorically. "The place was locked after the party."

"What was the party, anyway?"

"Bunch of bears," said Jason vaguely. He prided himself on his smooth sculpted body, which was the antithesis of a bear.

I remembered seeing a sign up about it. "The Bear Necessities party," I said, nodding.

"Whatevers," said Jason. "The point is, whoever was on the bar locked the pool when the party was over. You know that as well as I do. We're always careful about that. Barry *had* to unlock it. And there's no reason he'd unlock it just for himself." He glanced at me. "He didn't swim. You know that, right? He never learned. He didn't like the water."

"I know," I said. I felt miserable. Barry was dead and we were dissecting his life as though he were a character in a mystery novel. Barry had been real, and alive, and now he'd drowned and...

This time, I really did throw up.

Julie came by again after that. "Okay, Sydney," she said. "I know you told Pete and Celia already, but I want you to tell me, too. Everything from when you got here."

I told her. I told her about swimming on Sunday mornings and about how light the air

42

had felt as I cycled over to the inn. How I'd had nothing more weighty than marrying bears on my mind. How I'd had no premonitions of anything. How I hadn't even looked at the pool until I was ready to dive in. And how I had known, already, that Barry was dead, even though I didn't know how I knew that.

She nodded and took notes and didn't interrupt me and then at the end said, "Thanks. We're all set; you can go now."

"Just like that?" I stared at her. "So you know what happened?"

She shook her head. "Not yet. We'll have to see. The medical examiner wants to decline this one, but I'm insisting."

"What does that mean?"

She was still scanning the area. Outside the wrought-iron gate that led to the rest of the inn, curious guests were already congregating, looking concerned, murmuring together. It felt obscene. "It means they think that it's straightforward accidental," she said. "I'm not so sure."

"Why? What do you think?"

Her attention came back to me with a snap I could almost feel. "I couldn't speculate," she said. "But I want to find out more. I think it's important to be sure."

I nodded. Barry and Julie had been friends, too. In fact, I couldn't think of anyone Barry *wasn't* friendly with. "No one would kill Barry," I said.

"Let's hope not," said Julie.

6

The cop at the gate, one of the baby cops that P'town rents in the summer to help with traffic, held me up for a good five minutes as he laboriously took my name and address. I almost expected him to lick the end of his pencil. "Everyone knows me," I protested.

"I don't," he said officiously.

I cycled back to my apartment and stood under the hottest shower I could stand for as long as I could stand it, and I was still cold afterward. Ibsen chose that moment to be particularly annoying, rubbing around my ankles until I nearly tripped and fell, and I finally yelled at him. I *never* yell at Ibsen.

I thought for a while about who I could call. I have friends, lots of them, but they're like everyone else in P'town, working multiple jobs and exhausted in between. My mother was out of the question. My other best friend Mirela was in Bulgaria and never answered her phone when she was abroad. Ibsen had disappeared under my bed in a huff. And so finally, as though drawn there irresistibly, I went back to the inn.

And ran straight into Ali Hakim.

He'd gotten the sartorial memo, it seemed: today he was wearing khakis and a polo shirt. "Ah," he said. "Ms. Riley. I was hoping I could speak with you again."

"You're too late to arrest Barry," I said tartly, the words coming out of my mouth before my brain had time to engage. That happens to me a lot. "*So* sorry. I guess you'll just have to go bother other hard-working people. That's what you do, isn't it? Arrest people just for going about their daily business? Like being born American makes someone better than everybody else?"

It wasn't a new thought. I'd already experienced it on a smaller scale on the Cape: the assumption that being somewhere longer than someone else means one has more status than the other person. I know people—not close friends, mind you—who act as though having lived in Provincetown for 20 or 25 years is somehow a claim to fame, that it bestows something on the person that others lack. Magical pixie-dust, maybe.

Me, I think it's pretty sad if the only thing wonderful about you is that you've lived here a long time, but the issue comes up constantly. It's an aspect of exceptionalism, of course, but on the other hand I've been on the Cape long enough to see the damage wrought by recent arrivals who mean well, but who (because of their affluence and their usually unconscious arrogance) do a whole lot of damage. It helps me when I think about the current political climate in the States to at least partly understand nativism in all its ugliness.

Well, partly, anyway. This perceived superiority of those born in the US is still appalling. I'm sorry, but if you need to feel superior to someone else, pick another reason. Your birth in this country wasn't your doing. It was as much a matter of chance as it was for anyone else being born in another country. It doesn't make you stronger, smarter, or better.

One could argue that it made you a lot *luckier* than if you'd been born in South Sudan, for example, or Yemen. But luck isn't something to feel proud of. Feel gratitude for your luck, and maybe even try and help people from places where famine, genocide, war, and poverty are one's only birthright.

I climbed down off my mental soapbox and focused on Ali. He didn't respond to my words, but rather to what was behind them. His eyes grew darker, it seemed, and cloudy. "I know," he said gently. "I'm truly sorry for your loss."

I stared at him, the tears suddenly hot and pressing against my eyes. I dashed them away with the back of my hand. "No, you're not," I said. "Why should you be sorry? You didn't know Barry. Besides, you came to make trouble for him." I realized suddenly what I was saying. "Wait. You didn't by any chance come and make trouble for him last night, did you?"

We were standing in the reception area, and he glanced over at the front desk, where the ubiquitous Jason was unabashedly listening to us. "Coffee?" Ali suggested.

"Why not." I made it a statement rather than a question. I was struggling with too many emotions at once: loss, and anger, and suspicion. On a good day I'm lucky if I can handle one at a time. I let him guide me into the now-empty dining room and watched dully while he fetched coffee from the samovar. This time, he had a cup for himself too. So much for my ideas about exotic alternatives.

By the time he came back to the table I'd managed to get myself under control. A little, anyway. "Agent Hakim—"

"Ali," he suggested.

"Ali, then." I had bigger issues to quibble about than what I should call him. "You didn't answer my question. Were you harassing Barry last night?"

"We generally refer to it as interviewing," he said calmly. "And, as it happens, I wasn't. We had an appointment for this morning. That's why I'm here."

"Oh." I could feel the anger-energy draining from my body. "I found him, you know," I said miserably.

"I know." His voice was still gentle. "I'm sorry. I wish you hadn't."

"It was horrible." I was crying again, and he got up and brought me a couple of napkins from the coffee station and watched me dab at my eyes with them. "I'm sorry you had to go through that. I know you were friends."

I *so* didn't want to be crying in front of anybody, but especially not an ICE agent. If we'd met under different circumstances—well, okay, I'll be honest: it wouldn't have been any better then. Our current immigration policies seemed mean-spirited and cruel, and I pretty much made the assumption that the people who carried them out were the same. And here

I was, crying and letting him bring me what passed for tissues. It was all so second-rate soap opera. *Breathe, Riley. Just breathe.* "I'm fine," I snuffled.

"No, you're not, and you have good reason not to be," he said. His voice was still gentle. What was wrong with him? I peered around my napkin. "Why are you being so nice to me?" A thought drifted into my brain. "Are you hoping that I'll spill the beans about your investigation? Because, don't. There aren't any beans to spill." I took a shaky breath. "There's nothing to find out. Barry is dead and it's over. You should just leave, now." The thought of Barry set me off again.

Ali must have been accustomed to hostility in his line of work. He didn't leave. He sat there silently, not even drinking his coffee, while I went through a fresh paroxysm of tears. There was mascara all over the napkin. I couldn't imagine what my face looked like. I'd progressed to the hiccupping stage when Jason appeared in the doorway. "Mike was looking for you," he said, and then, taking another look at me, came over and perched on the settee beside me, his arm around my shoulders. "What are you doing to her?" he demanded. "What did you say?"

I turned and hiccupped into Jason's pristine shirt. "Not his fault," I managed to say, though why I was defending him, I hadn't a clue.

"If you want to talk to anyone here, talk to the manager," Jason said. "Not Sydney."

"It's okay," I said and reluctantly disentangled myself from him. Jason's sympathy—not to mention guard-dog tendencies—was threatening to bring on more tears, and I'd had enough of that. A deep, shuddering breath. "Thanks for the coffee," I said, to Ali, a little absurdly in view of the fact that he was in my space, not me in his. I stood up. "I have to go see—"

"—the manager," Ali finished for me. "I know." He looked at Jason. "And I really am sorry for your loss, for all of you. But I still have an investigation to conduct."

I stopped. "Not now!" I stared at him. "You were investigating *Barry*—"

"—and the Race Point Inn," he said smoothly. "I'm sorry, Ms. Riley, but—"

"Oh, for heaven's sake, this is P'town." This time I was the one to interrupt. "Call me Sydney, if you have to call me anything, if you're going to insist on staying around. Though we wish you wouldn't. No one uses last names here." I swear, it had sounded like a logical speech when it was inside my head.

Jason stood up and again put his arm protectively if a little dramatically around my shoulder, steering me toward the door. "I'll let you know when the manager can see you," he informed Ali. My last impression was of Ali standing there watching us go, a crumpled stained napkin in his hand, and the dark eyes cloudy and—if I wasn't mistaken—worried as hell.

Mike got straight to the point. "We have to move through this," he said briskly. "It's what Barry would have wanted." A quick glance as though to see if I were going to contradict him. Barry and I had been friends; with Mike, the relationship had been all business, and not always completely cordial at that. Barry loved the inn; Mike wanted it to be efficient. They weren't always the same thing. "We're fully booked through the end of the season, you have weddings, and there are some other events on the calendar..."

His voice trailed off as he moved restlessly to the window and looked out. The harbor stretched in front of him, dotted with little pleasure boats. There was a fast ferry coming in from Boston, rounding Long Point. "I don't know who owns the inn now," he said, "and that's not going to get clarified today or tomorrow. I don't even know how that works." He turned back to face me. "But I want it to be business as usual as far as the guests go."

"We'll have to drain the pool," I said. "No one's going to want to be in that water now." It had taken me half an hour of scrubbing to feel that it was all off of me.

"As soon as the police let us, we will. Meanwhile let's send guys to the Boatslip if they want a pool. But I want everybody feeling comfortable staying here."

"The police tape," I said, a little acidly, "might make that a tad difficult."

"Get with the program, Sydney," he said, irritated. "We'll work around all those obstacles. We have to work together. We have to present a united front."

"Against whom?" I asked. "The police? ICE?"

"The guests," Mike said.

***

I don't have a real office at the inn; Mike's the only one who does. My paperwork is done at an antique roll-top desk behind the reception area, and I was still sitting there a half-hour later, staring at my computer screen. Business as usual. Even the frigging ICE agent had been more sympathetic than Mike.

I tried to concentrate and then, watching the clock, stood up. "Cape Air flight's in in twenty minutes," I said to Jason. "I'm going to pick Glenn up."

"Oh, honey, are you sure?"

"Who else should go? Mike? *You?*" I didn't mean it to sound as harsh as it came out. "Maybe the police?"

He backed off, his hands up, simulating surrender. "Okay, okay, Wonder Woman. Knock yourself out."

"I'm sorry, Jason." I went and put a hand on his shoulder. "You're being so supportive. I didn't mean to snap."

"I know." He took my hand off his shoulder and kissed it lightly. "Go, and may the gods go with you."

Whoever that might be, I thought. I walked down the street to the big municipal parking lot at MacMillan Wharf and located my car in under two minutes, which had to be a new personal best. A Honda Civic that I referred to as the Little Green Car, having not come up with anything more original than that to name it. If it had been February, I could have made it out to the airport in about five minutes, but this was summer, Bear Week, and traffic crawled.

Bear Week. Did Barry's death have to do with visiting bears? I found that idea hard to get behind. Of all the theme weeks in town, this is my favorite. Unlike some of the other subsets, bears are nice. They're kind. They don't do drugs or get obnoxious or pass out in the street. They eat, they have parties (where they eat), they buy bear-related souvenirs and the special bear-claw pastries made specifically for their events, and almost without exception they're sweet guys. They're polite. They hold doors. They say please and thank you.

They're not known for drowning each other in closed swimming pools.

I crossed Route Six and headed out Race Point Road. The airport is located in the Cape Cod National Seashore, one of the most beautiful nature preserves in the country, comprising dunes, beaches, hills, and what amounts (on the Cape) to forest, with small trees stunted by the continuous wind. Everyone should take Cape Air to Provincetown sometime, flying over Boston's harbor islands and then out toward the open ocean, curving back in to line up for the airport approach, occasionally sighting whales coming to feed. I'd do it once a week if I could afford it.

The plane was on time and Glenn was just reclaiming his luggage when I got there. He's built on the rugged side, with an impressive beard that goes with his full, beaming smile. He has the most amazing collection of oversized t-shirts in the world. He likes pasta and Boston cream doughnuts.

And I was about to destroy his world.

"Sydney! That lazy bastard have you running errands for him?" He enveloped me in a—what else?—bear hug. "Good to see you."

"It's good to see you, too, Glenn." How do you break this kind of news? "I have the Little Green Car outside."

"Then let's go." He would fit in it, but barely. Suitcase in the back seat, Glenn struggling to get the seatbelt around him. I put the key in the ignition and turned to face him. "Glenn. I don't know how to say this, so I'm just going to say it. Barry's dead."

"What?" He was still smiling. He didn't think he'd heard me right.

"He's dead. He drowned last night in the pool at the inn." I reached out and put my hand over his. Maybe I shouldn't have been the one to do this. There were tears welling in my eyes already. It was too soon for me to talk about Barry without falling to pieces.

The smile was gone. "Barry's dead?"

I nodded and swallowed hard. "I'm so sorry."

"Barry's dead," he said again, his voice flat, lifeless. As lifeless as the body that had been floating in the pool. He sounded like he was trying out the words, feeling his way into his new reality. A reality that didn't include his life-partner. He turned and stared out the windshield. There wasn't anything to see there but sand dunes.

I took my hand back and turned the key in the ignition. "I'll take you there."

"No, wait." He reached over and turned the ignition off. "Tell me."

I swallowed again. "We don't know exactly what happened. Sometime last night, after the pool was closed up, he went out there. He must have fallen in." I paused. "He's never learned to swim."

"I know," he said. "I used to give him a hard time about it. Your two homes are on Cape Cod and Key West, and you can't swim." His voice faltered on the last word and he put a hand to his eyes. "Why the hell did he go out there after closing, the dumb bastard?"

"I don't know." My eyes were blurring with tears.

"Barry. Oh, God, Barry." This big man, this cliff of a human being, and what came out of him then was little more than a whimper. He was a little boy, suddenly, lonely and scared and in pain. The howling, I thought, would come later.

"I'm sorry, Glenn. I'm truly sorry."

He took a minute, and I tried to get hold of myself while he did. Finally he cleared his throat. "Um. It *was* an accident, wasn't it, Sydney?"

"What else could it be?"

He shrugged. "He has—he had—a history. Not now, not recently. But back in college. Decades ago, you know? He had a pretty serious suicide attempt." He teetered on the edge of losing it for a moment, got it back. "Pills. He took pills. Enough to overdose. Roommate got back early, called 911, they pumped his stomach. But…oh, God, never mind. I'm just talking. He wouldn't do that again."

"No," I agreed. "He wouldn't do that again. He was happy, Glenn. And he loved you. He wouldn't ever do that to you."

"No," he said, and this time there was an infinite sadness in his voice. "No, he wouldn't." He took a breath. "I'd like to go now."

"Of course." I started the car, pulled out of the parking lot, headed back toward town. Glenn was hunched over, watching out his window, his shoulders occasionally shaking gently. I didn't say anything until we pulled up at the inn. "I have to go park in the lot," I said, a little apologetically. As though Glenn needed an escort; the Race Point Inn had been his second home for over twenty years.

"Are you coming back?"

I nodded. "As soon as I park the car. I'll only be a few minutes."

"Okay." He fumbled his way out of the car, opened the back door, pulled out his suitcase, slammed the door, and then turned and looked up at the inn.

When I pulled away he was still just standing there staring.

7

I hadn't been entirely candid with Glenn. The truth was that Barry *had* talked to me about suicide. "It's about who decides," he'd told me one night over one margarita too many.

"Suicide is about despair," I pronounced carefully, with the absolute dogmatic certainty of the truly drunk.

"Suicide's about control," Barry said, shaking his head, disagreeing. "About deciding who gets to decide."

Somehow that had seemed funny to me and I'd burst out giggling, and he turned to me sternly. "You don't get to choose about being born," he said. "The only real choice that any of us has is choosing about when, and where, and how to die."

But here was the thing: If his life were truly wretched, Barry might have considered suicide; but what he absolutely, positively would never have done was choose water as his means of exit. Glenn had echoed him, eerily, when he talked about living on Cape Cod and Key West.

Barry always said that God had to have a sense of humor, to give him success and love in places that he would have normally have stayed away from. He hated water. He never even took baths, and his showers were quick. He didn't know how to swim and he didn't want to learn how to swim. His worst nightmares, he told me once, were about drowning. "That's the worst way to go. Imagine it, Sydney. You swim out and then you change your mind, only it's too late, and the water takes you."

I was thinking about that as I headed back into the inn. Never water. Pills, maybe. Had he taken pills before he fell in? But then why would he have gone into the pool area? He'd never have gone there alone at night. Would he? Had he?

As soon as I got to reception, Jason pounced. "He's here!"

"I know," I said. "I picked him up at the airport, remember?"

"Not *Glenn*!" He dismissed Barry's long-time companion with a wave of his hand. "Your Secret Agent Man."

"Oh, for God's sake," I said as Ali emerged from Mike's office. "You're still here?"

"And it's nice to see you as well," he said. "Believe me when I say that I'd prefer to leave you all to your grief."

Mike appeared in the doorway behind Ali. It was late enough in the day that he looked like he was trying to start a beard, but with only minimal success. "Sydney, can you come in here for a moment?"

It was with something of a feeling of being called to the principal's office that I trailed in after him. Ali stood aside and let me pass him, then followed me and shut the door behind us. Definitely a *déjà vu* of my school days.

It didn't help to see that all the paperwork spread out over Mike's desk was mine.

"Sit down, Sydney," said Mike, pointing to one of the chairs in front of his desk. Ali took the other one. I decided to go on the offensive. "Is this about his so-called evidence that we're marrying too many people who don't happen to be American?"

Ali didn't say anything. Mike cleared his throat. "I'm convinced," he said reluctantly, "that there's something to the accusation."

"You've got to be kidding! Mike, this is ridiculous. Barry would never—"

"Barry would," said Ali firmly. "And he did. I'm sorry, Sydney. But it's pretty clear that not all of the weddings you arranged were for love."

I looked at Mike. "What's he talking about?" Mike didn't answer.

Ali said, gently, "Mr. Parker was selling marriages. He's been doing it for a while, for years. Someone contacts him, someone who wants to get into the US, and Mr. Parker finds someone else who's a citizen here who's willing to tie the knot temporarily for a decent sum of money. The wedding goes through, the foreigner's on his way to a green card, and everyone's happy." He glanced at me. "We wondered if you weren't in on it, too, at first, but we've ruled you out."

"Gee, thanks," I said sarcastically. "That couldn't have been too difficult to ascertain. I wouldn't be living in the dump I'm in if I had that kind of cash." I stopped. "Wait. *What* kind of cash? How much money are you talking about? Because I haven't seen Barry living anywhere beyond his means."

He smiled. "We did check out your financials and where you live. We don't need to go into that now." He glanced over at Mike, who was sitting rigidly behind his desk, looking like he wished he could be anywhere else, doing anything more pleasant. Like, say, having a root canal.

Ali went on doggedly. "You must have seen you were booking a lot of people outside of the U.S."

"That's always the case." Man, was I feeling defensive. "Listen, this may come as a surprise to *you*, but not all countries share our commitment to marriage equality. Even if their marriage isn't recognized when they go home, some couples still want to make the commitment."

"But then they *don't* go home, do they?"

I sighed. "Maybe you don't want to believe this, either, but you know, it's entirely possible for people from two different countries to fall in love and want to build a life together. That's not completely out of the realm of possibility, is it?"

"Of course not. But that wasn't what he was doing," Ali said. "He started before you came on staff, Sydney, but your success was his success, too. Things really took off once you got here. With more weddings, he could run more scams."

"Wait—*is* it a scam?" I asked. "Look. He gives them what they want, right? Everyone's happy, no one's getting hurt. Unless you believe that I'm marrying a bunch of terrorists?"

"It's still against the law."

I shrugged. "So was smoking pot, until we changed that law."

"Okay. And when you change this one, I won't investigate anyone doing it."

I frowned. I still didn't believe that Barry had been doing *anything*. Maybe I didn't want to be convinced. "All right, so how did it work, this green-card scam of yours?"

"Not mine," he said, then saw my face and hurried on. "Okay. So Parker—"

"–Barry," I corrected him.

"–so Barry lined up some single people here. Possibly women, but mostly men, I think. Guys who were reasonably stable and who needed some decent money."

"That wouldn't have been hard to find," I said. Provincetown is feudal in some respects: we have two classes of people. The homeowners with the God-only-knows-how-many-million-dollar condos, and the seasonally employed, who are always on the lookout for affordable housing, of which there's precious little.

"Right. And so then all he had to do was spread the word that he had a nice little wedding package that included a five-year commitment and would cost enough to compensate the spouse on this end, and of course Mr. Parker himself."

"Spread the word how?"

He stared at me. "I thought you knew," he said. "That's part of why it worked so well. The H2Bs."

Of course. I felt like smacking my forehead. Every spring sees an influx of foreign workers into town, mostly Jamaicans and Bulgarians and Russians, a few Central Americans, South Americans, some others. My mother would have described them as "working all the hours that God gave them"; in other words, hard. They staffed hotels, boutiques, restaurants, clubs, tourist attractions…and the town wouldn't survive without them. Besides, as one restaurant owner was quoted a couple of years ago in the newspaper, "The American kids, when they apply for a job, their first question is when do they get their breaks. The foreigners' first question is, how many hours may I work?"

At some point somebody from each of these countries got a seasonal job—and a temporary non-agricultural worker's visa, called an H2B—and then went home and told all their friends and relatives about it, and before long we got a steady stream of young, bright, ambitious people coming to town every summer. They sleep—if they ever sleep, which I sometimes doubt—five to a room to save money, and they work hard. And, just as they spread word of their jobs to people at home, so too could they talk about this nice way to get a more permanent immigration status.

They probably wouldn't be the same people—I didn't see H2Bs being able to afford what Barry must have been charging—but the grapevine would see to it that those who *could* afford it heard about it.

"I get it," I said slowly. "So then they contact Barry and he matches them up with someone here who's in the market for the gig. But don't people have to actually *prove* they're married? Prove that they live together and everything?"

He nodded. "Yes, of course they do," he said. "Which means that the American would have to be paid very well indeed. It's a commitment. Two years in, the spouse can apply for resident status. Someone will interview the couple separately to make sure that they both give the same answers. Maybe a series of interviews."

"Like what? What are the questions?"

"Basically anything the agent thinks will catch them out," he said frankly. "What side of the bed do they sleep on? What did they have for dinner last Tuesday? What do they fight most about? Where do they keep the good china? Do their friends see them as a couple? Who gets up earlier than the other?"

"I get the point."

He shrugged. "We're not against people getting married who genuinely care about each other and want to build a life together, you know," he said.

"Right." I took a deep breath. "So how did you get on to Barry, if this is really what Barry was doing?

Mike roused himself. "*I'm* convinced," he told me. I ignored him.

Ali sighed and pulled a small notebook from his pocket. He flipped it open, glanced at a couple of pages. "You remember booking a wedding back in the spring for someone from Albania?" he asked.

I closed my eyes to see the calendar that's up over my desk at the inn. "Yes. Drinan and Pete." I never remember last names.

"Good memory." When I opened my eyes again, Ali was smiling. "And so you remember that they cancelled the wedding?"

I frowned. "Something about the travel arrangements not working out," I said.

"I'd say they didn't," said Ali. "What happened was, Drinan got to New York and was supposed to stay there for a few days with friends. Then come up here, meet his intended, have the wedding, and then back to the city where they would share an apartment for the statutory waiting period. Reality is, three days into it, he meets a girl in New York and they fall madly in love. P'town wedding cancelled; he'll find another path to a green card, probably through her."

"Okay," I said. I vaguely remembered the couple. Every season, at least one ceremony gets postponed or cancelled. I never think much about them. "So…?"

"So," he said, "Drinan had paid Mr. Parker a lot of money upfront. Probably in the neighborhood of ten thousand dollars, and that was just the down payment. He wanted it back." He paused. "There were, apparently, some threats."

I shook my head. "Isn't that motive for Barry to kill Drinan, not the other way around? Don't blackmailers become murder suspects?"

"I don't know anything about murder," Ali said. "I'm just telling you how this came to our attention."

"Anyway, it didn't have to mean anything," I said, taking another tack. "We do

weddings here that cost way more than that."
But I was remembering it, and I hadn't
booked this particular couple in for ten thousand dollars.

"Not this wedding. This wedding wasn't
going to cost much. This wedding was going
to be small, quick, intimate. Whatever your
base fee is. They weren't even staying here.
You got your deposit, and you probably even
refunded part of it. Mr. Parker's take was completely separate from yours."

I looked at Mike. He was inspecting his
fingernails. "That's all? You heard about one
possible case, and—"

"And then," he said smoothly, "there's
Diego Jimenez."

I frowned, thinking, and finally shook my
head. "I'm not placing the name."

"He did stay here at the inn, last summer,"
Ali said. "In the penthouse suite. He comes
from serious money in Caracas, an old Vene-
zuelan family. But Venezuela's economy went
bust and he didn't want to go down with the
ship." He glanced at his notebook. "It says
here that someone called *Lady Di* married him
to Spenser Callaghan? Is that right? Lady Di?"

"Local celebrity," I said. "Cross-dresser."

"I see." He obviously didn't. "Mr. Callaghan was cooperative and both men were in

fact gay, which apparently wasn't always the case, so it should have worked."

"What went wrong?"

"Not sure about the details, but there was one hell of a fight one night, mirrors shattering, people screaming, the whole nine yards. Stuff getting thrown out the windows. The police got called. This was up in Boston, where they were living. Eight months into the marriage and somebody turned them in and Diego got himself deported. And the first thing *he* did was turn Mr. Parker in."

"All right." I was suddenly too tired to argue. It was too much work to wrap my brain around that one—who turns someone in to the government out of pique? Another part of my brain was trying to understand that it was still Sunday, that it was just this morning that I'd come for my early swim and found Barry. It felt like a million years ago. "All right. But you can't arrest him now, unless ICE is more powerful than I thought and can reach past the grave. And you say you don't believe that I was in on it. So why're you still here?"

"Because," said Ali, "it might be why he was killed."

There was a very long pause. Finally I said, "You're not serious."

He raised an eyebrow. "Apparently the police are."

I looked at Mike. "Is that true?"

He lifted a hand, let it drop. He looked exhausted, too. "They've been asking if anyone wanted him dead," he said. "No one's said it, but that sounds pretty explicit to me."

I sat for a moment, then turned back to Ali. "I think," I said carefully, "that you'd better tell us everything.

***

It turned out that the reason Ali was aware of the Race Point Inn wasn't just because of these two irate customers. He'd been investigating for a couple of months already. He held out a pamphlet and I took it, astonishment overriding sorrow. "He had a *how-to manual*?"

The cover showed the inn and you couldn't fault the title for clarity: So You Want to Marry an American? I looked up at Ali. "Seriously? You'd think there'd be more of these going in the other direction."

Mike said, diffidently, "Canada's doing well on marriages these days."

"They probably have brochures, too." I leafed through the booklet and looked up. "I don't see anything in here that's illegal," I said. "I mean, maybe it's not too classy, right? A combination dating service and get-married-while-you-wait plan. But he's not saying that the marriages are fraudulent."

"Once you contact the email address," Ali said, "you get additional information. And screening. Mr. Parker was being very careful."

"Not careful enough, if you're here," I said. I really wanted to dislike this guy, but the thought of Barry using me to get rich was starting to make me feel a little queasy. Better not to know, maybe. *Breathe, Riley.*

Ali's voice went inexorably on. Barry had a vetting process, which was actually pretty impressive. Barry wasn't one to do anything by halves. There was paperwork. There were Skype calls. There were character references. And finally, there was the matchup. "The cost, you see," said Ali, "depended on the person here. How much it was going to disrupt their life to have a sham marriage for a while."

"How long, again?"

"Five years minimum to live together." He noticed my expression. "It's not as easy as people think. I suspect that Mr. Parker spent much of his time mollifying angry applicants." He took a deep breath. "First, let's get one important thing straight. Marriage to a U.S. citizen makes you eligible for a *green card*. That's all. Now, once you have a green card, you can apply for citizenship. But it's at best a two-step process. Partly, I would assume, to discourage business ventures such as this one."

I looked at Mike. "Tell me you didn't know about this."

"If he told anybody, it would have been you, Sydney."

I didn't want to think about that. I didn't want to think about our easy friendship, our confidences, the assumption I'd always made that we shared everything. It had all been a joke. "So even if the American sponsors you, you can't become a citizen?"

"Not right away," said Ali. "Having a green card for a certain number of years can make you *eligible* for U.S. citizenship. The spouse has to prepare a visa petition and you have to provide an application packet. A few months after that, we—by that I mean Customs and Immigration—call you in for an interview. If that goes well, you're approved for lawful conditional resident status. That's not even permanent resident status, because you presumably will not have been married for a full two years by the time your interview date arrives."

"So two years is the commitment?"

He shook his head. "Two years is the time period for you to be a conditional resident. And you have to live together all that time.

Neighbors, landlords, all those people are interviewed to make sure that you're living as a couple. Three months before the two years are up you put in a joint petition for permanent residence. That's the green card. And you still have to wait five years after you're given the green card to be eligible to apply for citizenship, and if you divorce in the meantime you go right back to illegal status and run the risk of being deported. So, all told, it's seven years that they're committed to the marriage, though they could reasonably live apart after four or five."

That sounded strangely Biblical to me. "I don't get it," I said. "You're asking someone to be with you in a relationship for seven years…there has to be a hell of a big incentive there. Who has that kind of money?"

"That's where it does get complicated," Ali acknowledged. "We believe that a number of the men—and it's been almost exclusively men—coming through Race Point have been connected to organized crime in their countries of origin. Sometimes it is in that country's best interests to see them gone."

"Oh, Jesus," said Mike.

"Not all of them," Ali said quickly. "There are other ways to obtain the funds. And it seems that Mr. Parker even had a payment plan of sorts with some of his—graduates. And others he let slide."

Barry and his big heart. "So what tipped you off? I mean, besides Drinan and Diego." It sounded like a vaudeville act.

"Right." He leaned forward in his chair, elbows on knees, and ticked some items off. "First, ever since gay marriage was legalized in Massachusetts, we've had our eye on Provincetown." He glanced at me. "Wedding Destination Central."

"Success has its price," I muttered.

"Just so. And the Race Point Inn seemed to be at the center of it all. Second, we had an agent try to come through the process himself." He grimaced. "Mr. Parker sussed him out right away before anything incriminating was said. He was astute."

Among other things. "But then you got the complaints?"

He nodded. "But then we got the complaints," he agreed. "What you might call sour grapes. There was something else—one of the marriages didn't work out. There was some sloppiness involved and the guy was turned down for his green card. He complained to us, we checked it out, but didn't find any evidence. All your couples seem to either live together in wedded bliss or else eventually divorce." He shook his head. "We've thought since then that something was going on here, but Mr. Parker was slick."

"Too slick," I said. "I had no idea." I was past the denial stage and well into feeling sorry for myself.

Ali was watching me. "It's a compliment, in a way," he said. "He probably thought you were too honest to work with him on it."

He and Mike were both looking at me. For possibly the first time in my life, I really didn't know what to say.

8

By the time I left Mike's office, I had a headache the size of Chicago.

The conversation with Ali had left me entirely disoriented. It wasn't so much that Barry had been running a green card scam out of Race Point Inn that was disturbing; it was that he hadn't trusted me enough to tell me. To know that even if I didn't approve, I'd never have turned him in for it. I don't have a Significant Other. I don't have parents I communicate with. What I had was Barry.

And Barry hadn't trusted me.

Ali was sympathetic but firm: there would have been a trial for sure, a prison sentence probably. Somehow, after all that, it hadn't felt as—hurtful, I guess—to hear that his death was being treated as suspicious. Jason supplied those details. "He's gonna be autopsied," he reported when I emerged finally from Mike's office.

"To find out that he drowned? That's not going to be helpful," I said. The headache was blinding. "Where's Glenn?"

"The police've been talking to him," said Jason. "They found out he inherits the inn. Can you believe that? He doesn't even *like* it here, and now he's going to be the new owner! Damn, what I could do with this place if it were mine!"

"Your grief is touching," I said with some asperity.

"Oh, honey, you *know* that I'm crying in my soul. But we have to look out for ourselves, don't we? It's not as if good jobs are all that easy to come by in this town."

"You're fine," I assured him. "Everyone knows the inn couldn't run without you."

"Well, there's that," Jason agreed.

I went outside and unlocked my bicycle. What I really needed was some fresh air and fresh faces and to get away from the sense that I was suddenly of the walls closing in on me. Alice Though the Looking-Glass time, I thought. Barry hadn't trusted me. Barry was running a green-card scam. Barry was being sued. Barry's death was suspicious.

Ali Hakim walked out into the small courtyard. There were three cars parked there—with only four spaces, guests pay a premium to keep their cars at the inn—and today they included an ostentatious Maserati (is there any other kind, really?) a Mercedes, and a classic Ford Mustang. He was unlocking the Mustang when he saw me watching him. "Can you recommend someplace for lunch?"

I checked my watch. Somehow it felt like years had passed, though it was only a little after three. "I guess I don't blame you for wanting to get away from the inn. We're known for suspicious deaths. Who knows what might be in the soup?"

He smiled and ignored my comment. "Good to get a little distance sometimes. And the police need the space." He hesitated. "You wouldn't want to join me, would you?"

"For more interrogation?"

"For lunch," he said firmly.

Why not? I locked the bicycle again and went around to the passenger side of the car; he leaned through and unlocked the door. "Wouldn't have figured you for a muscle-car guy," I remarked.

"Actually," he said, "it belongs to my sister. I don't own a car, and she doesn't use hers much, so I end up with it when I need to go out of town. Which way?"

"Sorry?"

"To lunch. Which way?"

"Oh." I thought quickly; there aren't that many restaurants you can access via a car. I directed him to Mac's Fish House on Shank Painter Road and we managed to score both a parking place and a table, a minor triumph during Bear Week. "So where is it you live that you don't need a car?" I asked.

"Boston. Really. I sold my car when I got transferred back home from DC. Public transport is excellent, and the agency gives me a car if I need one."

"Just not a Mustang," I said and smiled.

"Just not a Mustang," he agreed.

We ordered sushi—Mac's has, hands down, the best and freshest sushi on the Cape—and one of those awkward pauses ensued. That was when it hit me. My best friend had died under suspicious circumstances, and now here I was on a date with the guy who had come to arrest him. It doesn't get much more absurd than that. And we'd just ordered: there was no escape now.

Might as well face it head-on. "This feels awkward," I said. "Being with you here—and you investigating…"

"I'm just trying to tie up the loose ends," Ali said. "I'm talking with Glenn Rogers later this afternoon. He needs to know that there's an investigation pending, but the rest can wait. He has enough to deal with. I'll head back to town after that."

If it wasn't ridiculous, I would have felt a stab of disappointment. "So just like that? It's over?"

"It's never really over," he said, taking a sip of water. "We'll keep a file—we never get rid of a file. We're paid by how many kilobytes of data we can amass." A quick glance. "All right, so that wasn't funny, but it's also close to the truth. We'll coordinate with whomever ends up investigating Mr. Parker's death. But unless it's clear that the new owner is continuing the scam—well, we have other business."

"I know you have," I said grimly. "I've wondered a lot since the election how ICE agents manage to sleep at night." We all said it that way, like it was capitalized: The Election. "And don't say that you don't make policy, you're only carrying it out, either. That's an argument that didn't work at Nuremberg."

His gaze was mild; I expect that he had heard it all before, over and over again. "I don't deport people," he said quietly. "I investigate people like your boss who are scamming the system."

"Your agency deports people."

"Our *country* deports people."

"Some of us think that we shouldn't."

The sushi arrived. I could feel my cheeks flush. We waited in silence while the plates were put down and the waiter hovered. I fidgeted with my chopsticks for a moment. "All right. I'm sorry. You're not personally responsible for what the administration does."

"We need policy changes," he said. "Speaking as an individual, I agree about the administration. And for a while I've believed that I could create change from within. At least see that some of the investigations—my investigations—were done properly and not with an agenda behind them." He shrugged. "Lately, I've been less sure of that."

"Wow. A federal agent with a conscience." As soon as the words were out of my mouth I wished I hadn't spoken them. Why did I feel such a need to be mean to this man? "It must be difficult," I said, to take the edge off it.

"It must have been difficult," he said, "to hear me tell you those things about your friend."

"It was," I said. I played with my Cape Cod roll for a moment and then looked up. "You're sure about what you said back there? That Barry's death wasn't an accident?"

He swallowed a bite of his sashimi, took another sip of water. "Not my department, but from what I gathered, yeah, it sounds suspicious. The medical examiner will make the determination, of course." He must have seen the consternation on my face, because he said, quickly, "That's just procedure, Sydney. They need to determine the cause and manner of his death."

"Cause—and manner?"

"Cause of death is what made the heart stop beating. A gunshot wound, for example. Manner of death is how it happened—natural, or accidental, or through suicide or homicide." He looked at me unhappily. "You don't really need to think about this now," he said. "They'll be running toxicology tests for sure, so it's going to take a while for them to determine what happened."

"How long?"

A shrug. "Weeks, maybe? Maybe less: there's an office of the medical examiner in Sandwich, so Mr. Parker's remains aren't being sent to Boston. Boston has a backlog right now...well, Boston always has a backlog." He took another bite. "You were right, this is excellent."

"But how can we do anything in the meantime?" I demanded. "Glenn has to make plans. There has to be a funeral. And...well, I know that you're pussyfooting around saying it, but honestly, if someone murdered Barry, I know we'd all rather know that, and know who did it."

Ali touched his napkin to his lips. "Would that it were that simple," he said, and then sighed. "I could make a call," he said cautiously. "No, don't get excited, I have no idea if it would help or not. But agencies—some of them, anyway—sometimes cooperate." He hesitated. "And then there's my sister."

"Oh, yes? And who's your sister?"

A faint smile. "Commissioner, Boston Police Department," he said.

"Oh."

"Oh, indeed."

"She's the one who owns the muscle car."

"And lends it to me, since she gets driven everywhere."

We smiled at each other. "Well," Ali said at length, "I can ask."

"Please do. I can't stand the thought of waiting for weeks to find out what happened to him."

"Well, the investigation will continue, no matter when the lab results come in. But they'd be better off with knowing what the results are."

"When's the…autopsy?" I was pretty certain I'd never ever said that word before.

"Tomorrow. In Sandwich." He caught my look. "They won't keep him long, Sydney. You'll be able to go ahead with the funeral. They remove what they need for the testing."

"I am never," I said clearly, "inviting you for sushi again."

The quicksilver smile. "I make a great first impression, don't I?"

"Impressive beyond words. Now let's talk about rainbows and unicorns so I can enjoy this."

He dropped me back at the inn; I had no idea where he was off to. What I wanted more than almost anything in the world was to go home, to soak in a very *very* hot tub with scented water, and to drink about half a bottle of red wine. What I did, on the other hand, was go looking for Glenn. Jason might be about ensuring his future employment; I was about giving Glenn a shoulder, should he need one.

Jason was talking to a group of bears— *what's a group of bears called, anyway?* I used to know a bunch of venery terms, for a pub quiz group I led for a while, but it didn't come to mind. A roar of bear? A hibernation of bear?

And then I remembered: a sleuth of bear. Under the circumstances, what else could it be?

Glenn was sitting by the pool, alone. It was still taped off and locked up, but the police didn't seem to have a problem with him being there, so I joined him, dragging a chair over next to his. "Hey, Glenn."

He glanced up, then looked back down to the water. He was actually stroking his beard. I don't know that I'd ever seen anyone doing that. "Sydney."

I cleared my throat. "I suppose—I mean, I know how inadequate this is, but I'm really so so sorry, Glenn."

"Thanks."

We sat for a few moments in silence, just watching the pool. "He hated the water," Glenn said finally, stopping his OCD self-grooming. "It's like maybe at some level he always knew that's how he'd end."

"I'm sure he didn't mean for it to happen here," I said. "Or now. Glenn, you know—Barry loved you very much."

"Yes," he said pensively. "Yes, I suppose he did. Not exactly faithful until death did us part…"

"He was," I said. "In his own way." The terms of their relationship hadn't been particularly secret: sex with other men when they were away from each other was fine, but *verboten* when they were together, unless a threesome was agreed upon. It wasn't a particularly

87

unusual arrangement and seemed to work for
a lot of couples, married or not.

"He wasn't," he said. "In any way."

I stared at him. "Glenn—"

"Oh, I know about the pickups," he said,
waving a hand dismissively. "We both did it.
What do you think Key West looks like in the
winter? Completely target-rich environment.
No; this was different."

"What happened?"

For a moment, I thought he wasn't going
to tell me. But then he drew in a deep shuddering breath, as though making a decision.
"There was someone," he said. "Someone
here, someone he—liked. Listened to.
Quoted."

"A friend—" I began and he held up his
hand. "Don't insult me, Sydney. And don't try
to smooth it over. I think this is a good time
for us all to be honest, don't you?"

I nodded. "I didn't know," I said.

"I know. He only told me recently. He said
that keeping it secret from me was killing him.
Tearing him apart. He said they were close,
but he didn't say how close, and I didn't ask.
Just that he was seeing someone was doing a
number on his head."

"Someone here? Someone from P'town?"

He shook his head. "I don't know. Probably. Or maybe someone coming for Bear

Week. I don't know. I feel like I didn't know much about him, after all. He said they were talking every day. It must have been about their relationship; what else would it be?"

"Glenn. I'm sorry." I wanted to touch him but didn't know how. "You didn't know? You had no idea?"

He shook his head, like a bull that's been pierced too many times in the arena. Like a bear being baited. "Is there anything I can do?" I asked softly, inadequately.

He shook his head again. I reached over then and took his hand and held it tight as he burst into tears and cried and cried and cried.

And I sat and listened to him and thought that if this new person, this new bear thought that Barry was going to choose Glenn (and of course he was going to choose Glenn), then we had another candidate for someone who might wish Barry ill.

For such a nice guy, the list of people who might want him dead was growing by leaps and bounds.

9

And so endeth the first night.

By the time I got out of the inn it was dinnertime, a steady stream of people flowing into the restaurant, the streets forming their own currents of humanity. Mike did the managerial thing: got the staff together and told them that Barry was dead—though his word to describe what had happened was "accidental"—and reassured them that for the moment at least it was life as usual.

No one had time to dwell on it; summer season is like that. The pressure of working with a demanding public, combined with the pressure of making as much money as possible in the shortest period of time as possible, meant that there wasn't space in anyone's head for gossip or speculation. There may have been some hurried conjecture in the kitchen among the pots and pans, but it would have been curtailed quickly: Adrienne needs to be everybody's focus, at every moment, and her ego wouldn't allow people to talk about anyone but her.

Mike issued a press release as well, so that at least the Cape and Boston papers would carry news of Barry's death. There were so many people to think about notifying: the inn's regular clients, the organizations to which Barry belonged…and then, of course, there were the shadow people, the weddings that weren't really weddings at all.

I'd finally grabbed my wedding calendar and laptop and taken them home with me: I really needed some uninterrupted time. I put on a ragged t-shirt and shorts and the sloppy socks that I find comforting, made myself a cup of herbal tea (I really hate the stuff, but I didn't think I needed any more stimulation today), and spread out on the couch and coffee table. My mission was to figure out which of the slew of upcoming weddings—and we had about thirty of them on the schedule—were part of Barry's special project.

Ibsen tried to curl up on the papers and I pushed him away enough times that he finally got the hint and perched on the back of the sofa as if surveying my work. "What do you think?" I asked him. "Are they really here?" Ibsen does this weird thing when he's thinking, opens his mouth slightly so that just the tip of his tongue protrudes. He was doing it now.

Part of me didn't want to find anything; part of me wanted to be able to take out the card that Agent Ali Hakim had left with me and call him and proclaim that he was way off-base with his accusations.

And part of me had a bad feeling that he wasn't.

I divided the upcoming weddings into two categories: those with both sides of the couple coming from the US, those with one member outside of it. That alone was problematic: despite the fact that there's a flow of communication between us in preparation for the event, I don't always get the full 411 on both partners. The Commonwealth of Massachusetts doesn't require identification cards to be presented when the couple applies for their license; it doesn't require a witness; it's basically all about if you pay the fee and follow the right procedure, you're good to go.

That procedure is a little archaic in that couples must apply for the license in person and then wait three days before picking it up—again, in person. A throwback, I've always thought, to the days of shotgun or coerced marriages; or maybe so that somebody doesn't get completely drunk and wake up married. I'm not exactly sure how waiting three days is supposed to help with the former, though it could with the latter for sure.

And even so, the waiting period can get waived. It's not convenient, but a couple can travel to Orleans or Barnstable and petition a judge to allow them to marry on the same day. It's costly but rather fun—these judges are tired of the same DUIs and minor drug-possession charges that are their daily grind; they generally find the couples applying for a waiver delightful.

Aside from that, though, no one has to declare anything about themselves. The town clerk—and Provincetown has the most delightful town clerks imaginable, both of them—takes names, parents' names, date and place of birth, current address, current occupation, the name they want to use after they're married, and Bob's pretty much your uncle.

So just having been born outside of the US doesn't mean anything. And if the current address is Ukraine or Romania or Gabon, that doesn't really mean much, either. Most people applying to get married are already living together, but some few couples still seem to do it the old-fashioned way and put the wedding before the moving van.

I sifted through my notes. I have my own questionnaire—turns out that the facility providing the wedding needs a lot more information than does the Commonwealth—and that was where the problems would turn up. If indeed there were any to turn up.

I always ask couples how they met, and how long they've been together. Neither of those answers has a direct bearing on the wedding, but I like to have a sense of who they are, and sometimes I can alter decorations or food choices or something of the sort to go with their backgrounds and preferences that even they hadn't been aware of.

Besides, it's just plain fun. I love hearing all the different stories, from accidental encounters to set-ups, from online dating sites to old flames re-ignited. I've overseen the weddings of people who had been together a couple of months and of people who were marking their 63rd anniversary as a couple. And they all have a story to tell.

So now I started a new pile of folders: couples who had been together for under a year. It made sense that if you're entering into a marriage of convenience, you don't try it out for very long first. And the pile grew. And grew. And these were the people who had answered truthfully; there were probably a lot more that belonged in that pile. There was no reason, after all, to tell me anything they didn't want me to know.

I looked at the papers in sick fascination. What kept nagging at me was that I probably would never have caught it, never have seen that anything was wrong, because we do so many weddings in a season. And these were spread out among them, hidden as it were in plain sight.

The first ones started soon after I'd started my job, three years ago. Raul and Peter; Raul from Colombia, Peter from Milwaukee, known each other a month. Jeffrey and Michael; Jeffrey from Baltimore, Michael from Croatia, together a blissful three weeks. And it wasn't just gay couples: Mindy from Miami didn't just have a little alliteration going, she'd also had had a scant week before realizing it was true love with Etienne from Tunisia.

The other tipoff? These were all small weddings with few to no guests, and they were all taking advantage of the most basic wedding package we offered. Cheaping out, as we say in the business.

I looked at Ibsen. "Have I been really stupid here?" His tongue was still sticking out; that told me everything I needed to know. I gave it up, took a sleeping pill, and went to bed.

***

The next day I was at my desk behind reception when the inn's landline rang and Jason answered. "Sure, she's here, no problem." He hit the hold button. "It's your boyfriend, line two."

"I don't have a boyfriend," I said.

"You just keep telling yourself that, honey."

I sighed and picked it up. "Sydney Riley."

"Did you know," said the voice on the other end, "that Sydney Riley was the name of a famous spy in the early 1900s?"

"He spelled it differently," I said. "Good morning to you, too."

Ali laughed. "One wonders what your parents were thinking," he said.

I actually wondered about a *lot* of things that my parents had been thinking at different times in my lifetime; my attempts to get a grip on it all had for some time kept a local psychotherapist in business. "Tell me that you didn't just call for a chat about espionage history."

"No, though it might have been fun. My sister moved your friend's autopsy up and they're putting a rush on the results."

"Friends in high places," I said, then remembered to add, "Thank you, Ali."

"All part of the service. Wouldn't want you thinking that ICE is completely heartless."

"Where, oh where would I ever have gotten that idea?"

"Be nice, and I'll call you as soon as I get the results."

"Thanks," I said, a little awkwardly. It's a difficult balancing act, insulting someone while asking for their help. "Ali—why are you doing this for me?" It wasn't as though I had any official standing here, and there were favors being called in for sure. Even I could figure out that the medical examiner in Sandwich didn't report to the police commissioner in Boston.

"Told you. Wanted to let you know that there are at least a few of us who try to be sure we can sleep at night." He coughed. "Sorry. I'll let you know as soon as I hear anything."

"Thanks," I said, and softened my voice a little. He was, after all, going out on a limb for me. "I really appreciate it."

I disconnected and heard someone clear his throat. Jason. He was smiling broadly. "*What?*"

"Nothing, Sydney."

"Don't do impish," I said. "It doesn't become you. And I have work to do."

"Of course you do, Sydney."

Mike was in the office doing not much of anything. "This isn't happening," he said when I came in.

I sat down on the arm of one of the guest chairs. "I know," I said. "It feels unreal, doesn't it? Like Barry's going to come walking in at any moment." That was how I was trying to imagine him, anyway. Not as I had seen him last, floating in the pool, his face screwed up in a mask of agony.

"It's not just Barry," he said. "It's Glenn."

Glenn. I should go and see him, I thought. I wondered if he was going to track down Barry's other guy, and what kind of ugly scene might ensue. I wondered who Barry's other guy had been, come to that. No one he'd brought to Race Point, that was for sure. I hadn't had an inkling. No one had had an inkling. Poor Glenn, I thought. "Poor Glenn," I said out loud.

"Poor Glenn?" Mike sounded incredulous. "Poor us, you mean. Barry hasn't been dead more than a day and Glenn's already got his fingers in the inn."

"Well, he's technically co-owner," I said uncertainly. "And he'll be full owner for sure once…" My voice trailed off. I couldn't say the words. Unless, of course, he was the one who'd murdered Barry. Which he wasn't. *Breathe, Riley.*

"And he's already showing us who's boss," said Mike.

"Why? What's going on?"

"It's July," said Mike. "It's Bear Week. We're overrun. No one's getting any sleep. And he's got an auditor coming in this afternoon. How the fuck he got an auditor on this short notice…"

"An auditor? Why?"

"Well, it's not because he thinks that everything's just peachy here at the inn," Mike said.

I stared at him. "Something's wrong with the books?"

He threw up his hands. "I don't know, do I? Do I look like a bookkeeper? Do I look like an accountant?"

"Then just ask…" I stopped. "Oh."

"*Oh* is right," he agreed gloomily

We'd had a bookkeeper, right up until the season began in June, at which point she had decided that what she really wanted to do in life was go to medical school. In *June* she had decided this. And a cursory look at her work showed that it was just as well she was changing vocations. Either that, or she'd simply let everything go while fantasizing about doing surgery. The books were a mess, and hiring someone in the summer was dreaming the impossible dream. I'd completely forgotten; I do my own invoicing for the wedding work.

"But there's nothing wrong," I said now. "Everything's a mess, yeah, but come October we'll hire someone and they'll figure it all out."

"Except that Glenn wants it figured out now. He thinks there's money missing somewhere. A lot of money, he said."

"That's nonsense." I took a breath. "That's impossible."

"Tell it to Glenn. I don't need this," Mike said peevishly. "I really, really don't need this."

I stood up; what *I* didn't need was to listen to him whine. "And Barry didn't need to die, did he?" I asked. "Get a grip, Mike."

"Close the door on your way out."

Well, I was off to a great morning of making friends and influencing people. But all of this was coming together in an ominous way. If you'd asked me a week ago what shape the Race Point Inn was in, I'd have laughed. One of the most popular inns in Provincetown. Consistent heads in beds, as the hotel saying goes. Great staff, excellent facilities. Amazing ratings on sites like Trip Advisor and Yelp. A world-class dining experience.

But now it seemed there'd been cracks that hadn't shown through all of that. The stellar wedding business had been at least partially a front for a green-card scam. There might be some significant money missing, somewhere. Barry hadn't just been availing himself of one-night stands in his open relationship but had had a secret lover as well. Nothing was as it had seemed.

And it occurred to me that any of those secrets could have led to violence. Suicide, perhaps.

Or murder.

10

Jason hailed me as soon as I emerged from the office. "So, did you hear the latest?"

"That depends on what the latest is," I said guardedly. With Jason, one never knew.

"We're being sued!"

Okay, so that was new. "You don't have to look so happy about it." I perched on the stool we keep behind the reception desk.

"Well, I don't know if Barry took you into his confidence about this or not—" he looked left and right dramatically, lowered his voice, and leaned in "—but he had plans to add on another eight rooms, right above the restaurant!"

I shrugged. Barry *hadn't* told me, in point of fact, and I wasn't so grown-up that I didn't experience a moment of petulance over it. "So?"

"So the condo association next door doesn't want it to happen," Jason said. "I heard all about it at dinner last night. Honey, the trustees there are *hard-core*. They were going to take him to court!"

"Well," I said, "then they'll be pleased that Barry's not here anymore to build the extra rooms."

"But don't you see?" He paused dramatically. "Maybe one of them came over night before last? And had a few drinks with Barry to smooth things over after the party? And then pushed him in the pool?"

"Jason," I said wearily, "Provincetown is filled with condo associations at war with other condo associations or businesses. No one's resorted to murder over it."

"Not yet," he said, nodding knowingly. "Personally, I'd have loved the extra rooms. More tips."

"You do pretty well already," I said. Everyone loved Jason. The men loved flirting with him. The women loved his sometimes over-the-top attention. I'd seen some of his tips, and I'd have been thrilled with them.

He shrugged. "You know how money is, honey. There's never enough of it."

The mail carrier breezed in. "Hey, Race Point People." He thumped down a stack of envelopes.

"Thanks, Chris," I said to him, as Jason began leafing through the letters. "Bill…bill…here's one for you, Sydney…bill…ad…"

"I don't actually need to hear a description of everything," I said, taking the envelope and slitting it open. A deposit for a wedding in October.

"Nothing for me," he finished, disappointment in his voice. I looked up from the check. "You think a lot of people write letters addressed to the guy in reception?"

"You'd be surprised." He caught sight of the check in my hand. "Now, I could do with a few of those."

I pushed myself down off the stool. "Stop bitching, Jason," I said. I put the check and letter in the locked drawer of my desk and headed off to the dining room. I needed a coffee like nobody's business.

My smartphone rang while I was still pouring it. "Sydney Riley."

"Okay, so we heard that there are police all over the place there and there's been someone killed and we're freaking out a little here."

I took a deep breath. "Who is this?" I asked. The way things were going, I reflected, it could have been anyone.

"Sarah Millson. Of course."

Of course. Sarah Millson was scheduled to get married next Friday. To a man who was Boston Brahmin through and through. There's a relief, anyway, I thought suddenly: no green-card issues here. I thought I'd heard that he had an ancestor on the Mayflower. And Sarah herself had actually been a débutante; yes, that was apparently still a thing, who knew? Why they'd chosen Provincetown as a wedding venue was still a mystery to me. "Hi, Sarah."

"I can't believe this. I can't believe that there's a problem. Why did it have to be this week?"

I bit back a couple of possible responses. Yeah, Barry was that inconsiderate. So sorry he had to die the week before your wedding. The Millson wedding had been planned a year in advance and I'd gotten pressure from Barry to take it on. Not for the first time I found myself wishing I'd stuck to my guns. "It won't affect anything for you," I said, soothingly. "The police will be gone by next week and the pool will be open again."

"But it was in the *newspaper*!" It was a wail. Sarah Millson wasn't accustomed to events not bending to her wishes.

"And it will be old news by next Friday," I said, hoping that was true. "Everything's all set, Sarah, I promise you that everything will be fine. Better than fine."

It had better be, I thought. The fiancé had been firm. He had, I remembered hazily, some connection with the Race Point Inn. Probably something from before the time when Provincetown became a gay destination. I'd made them come and meet with me, just so that they could see with their own eyes what the town was like, and neither of them seemed particularly bothered. It was in the details that wedding devils surfaced, anyway, and Sarah's wedding was no exception. She wanted to audition CDs from five different string quartets (I don't think there are five different string quartets on the Cape). She changed her mind about the cake about—oh, I don't know, eighty-three times. She complained about her gown (for the record, I have absolutely nothing to do with wedding gowns), the menu (Adrienne started having steam coming out of her ears), and even the weather ("but what if it's too hot?").

I get spoiled working in Provincetown. Most people who want to get married here are less into the ceremony and more into each other. We're casual, and they *get* that. They're flexible and excited that they're tying the knot. I have to thank my lucky stars that I only get Sarah Millsons once or twice a season.

But she was right about one thing: the timing sucked. Having the most difficult wedding of the summer the week after the inn's owner is killed wasn't exactly convenient for me, either.

"Barry" and "killed" still didn't belong in the same sentence.

I went in search of Glenn. I couldn't get a read on him: he was reeling with grief one moment, freaking out about having a rival the next, and then checking the account books and claiming there was money missing after that? It made no sense. Maybe it's not supposed to make sense—I don't, after all, have all that much experience of loss and how people respond to it—but I thought that it would be worth seeing if there was anything I could do for him.

And, of course, there was a small voice in the back of my mind echoing Jason's concerns: when the dust settled, it was Glenn who was going to be our new boss, for better or for worse. I wasn't particularly *proud* of that voice, mind you; but I listened to it.

The first thing that I noticed was that the police had taken down the crime-scene tape, and the pool was open again. And doing a bang-up business for it still being before noon, with bears (and a few less-hairy companions) in the water, on the lounge chairs, at the outdoor bar. Life goes on, I thought. By the next time the bears were in town—for the Spooky-Bear Halloween celebration—it would seem as though Barry had never been here at all.

And there were tears in my eyes again at the thought. So there were things he'd been into that he hadn't shared. So he'd been maybe (and I wasn't about to automatically assume his guilt without proof) less than honest. Who doesn't have secrets? And in the meantime, Barry was gone. He wouldn't be here for Spooky-Bear. He wouldn't be here for anything—late-night chats, laughter and joking around the inn, the way he listened, really listened, when you had something to say. His bear hugs.

Glenn was in the dining room, sitting at one of the tables by the window, deep in conversation with Martin. "Sorry, am I interrupting?"

They both looked up at me, Martin with his usual stiff smile—there wasn't anything relaxed about Martin, not ever—and Glenn with a distracted look on his face, as though he wasn't really seeing me, as if he were doing sums in his head. "Sorry?"

"Just wanted to see if there's anything I can do for you."

Martin looked pained. He and I have always had something of an uneasy working relationship; I plan events and he oversees them, and we don't always have the same ideas about how things should go. Someone had once called Martin "snooty," though not to his face; I thought it was a marvelous description. Physically he was handsome—you really do have to be handsome in P'town, unless you're a bear; they have different standards—with dark wavy hair just starting to turn slightly silver, and the chic-est of chic eyeglasses. And then there was that expression, as though he was permanently smelling something that didn't quite smell right. Martin looking pained was Martin at his most usual self.

Glenn finally focused on me. "Sydney," he said. "I still can't really believe it."

"We're working on the funeral reception," Martin informed me, in an obvious bid to get me to go away.

"It's hard to believe," I said, ignoring Martin. "I woke up this morning and it was a couple of minutes before I remembered."

Glenn nodded. "That's exactly it," he agreed, and then his gaze sharpened. "Have you heard anything?"

"From whom?"

He waved a pudgy hand. "Anyone. Anyone who knows anything. People talk to you, Sydney."

Martin cleared his throat. Martin liked to think that people talked to *him*. I ignored him. "As soon as I do, I'll tell you," I assured Glenn, not entirely truthfully. Whatever Ali managed to find out might not be something that Glenn would want to know. There's truth, and then there's tact.

I've always erred on the side of tact.

Glenn didn't seem to have anything else to say, so I left them. If it were a normal day with no weddings to organize, I'd have probably spent it on Commercial Street, drifting around, seeing people I knew, maybe getting something to eat at the Aquarium Mall and a drink to go with it at the Aqua Bar, watch the boats scudding around in the harbor. Somehow, that didn't feel quite right to me today. I didn't have anything to do at the inn, yet I was loathe to leave it. As though something momentous might happen in my absence.

Well, it wasn't as if a lot *hadn't* been going on beneath the surface. I hadn't picked up on any of the undercurrents that had apparently been swirling around the inn. Sometimes I knew there was something there—after all, Provincetown was just like any other place: two different people could live there at the same time and yet experience two completely different P'towns. There were subcultures galore. The visual artists all knew each other and moved in the same gallery-and-studio circles. The kids who were fellows at the Work Center all stayed together and despised everyone else. The people from the Center for Coastal Studies tended to hang out at the Squealing Pig or the OC. The fishermen and the remnants of the old Portuguese families all did things connected to St. Peter's church and didn't eat out at all. And that didn't even scratch the surface of the multiple gay subcultures.

I knew that since I didn't belong to any of these groups—I'm a bit of an anomaly here— that there was a lot that went on of which I was completely unaware. I knew that there were a lot of people awake and doing things when Ibsen and I were long asleep. I knew that there were language barriers, physical barriers, cultural barriers that separated us all, as much as on the surface we seemed to be one happy carefree family. And I knew, even with Barry, even with Jason, that my not being a gay man excluded me *de facto* from a lot of things.

But I'd never suspected just how deep those differences ran. Maybe I was naïve. Maybe I was just stupid.

On that happy thought, I said to hell with it, went home and collected my swimsuit, got in my car, and went out to Herring Cove Beach. Some days you just have to stop your brain from going round and round and round.

11

I woke up the next morning with the Hangover From Hell.

I say "woke up," but that sounds like something relaxed and gentle, and it couldn't be further from the truth. I did not ease into this good day. I didn't set the alarm on my smartphone to snooze. I didn't even surface slowly from the gossamer bits of half-remembered dreams into the reality of my hangover.

No: I was awakened by a pounding on my front door. Possibly the worst way to re-enter consciousness when you feel like I felt.

I reached out for my phone and blinked blearily at it; the numbers blinked blearily back. It was either seventy-eight o'clock or nine-thirty Fahrenheit; I didn't much care which. There was a renewed attack on the door. I slid out of the bed and went straight down to the floor, feeling around me for something to cover up the t-shirt and shorts I normally sleep in during the summer, then realized I was still wearing the sundress from last night. Oh, shit. "I'm coming!"

I managed to pull myself up and staggered into the living room, pushing my hair up and away from my face. Touching my head set off a whole new set of shooting lights and pain.

Ibsen added his strident voice to all the other noises ricocheting around my skull. "I'm never having a drink again," I told him. He was unimpressed. He'd heard that one before.

Third time banging at the door. I was going to commit a murder myself if they didn't stop. I left Ibsen still yelling at me and made my way to the door and opened it. "What?"

Julie Agassi was standing there. "Sorry to wake you, Sydney. We tried calling."

"Uh-huh." I said intelligently. "Um—who's we?"

She moved slightly so I could see the man standing behind her. Another suit. He looked fresh and *very* not hung over. "This is Dennis Ramirez. He's from the district attorney's office. I told you I'd be calling them."

"Yeah. Okay," I said.

"Can we come in?"

I sighed and took a step back, opening the door wider. "By all means."

I let them come in and find a place to sit, or stand, or whatever the hell it was they wanted to do. I stumbled over to what my real estate agent had euphemistically called the kitchen, leaned over the sink, and splashed some water on my face. I filled a glass and drank it down; pity I hadn't considered drinking water last night. I straightened the dress, pushed my hair out of my face again, and turned to face my company, leaning against the counter.

Julie didn't look unsympathetic; I've had a beer or two with her at The Pig, and she could probably feel a little of my pain. She inched forward on my sofa. "It's about Barry," she said.

Since I don't normally have cops and lawyers banging on my door, even with my hangover I had just about managed to gather that impression on my own. "Yes?"

Dennis Ramirez cleared his throat. "This has officially become a murder inquiry," he said.

"Right."

"You don't seem terribly surprised."

"You're here, aren't you?" My voice seemed incredibly loud. "I assume that the autopsy got fast-tracked by the Boston commissioner and something showed up there." I looked at him as a thought formed itself reluctantly in my brain. "Are you here because you suspect me?"

"We're talking to everyone," Julie said. She had taken out a notebook. "The last time you saw Barry before you found him in the pool was late in the afternoon on Saturday, right?"

I nodded. I turned and opened a drawer or two until I found the aspirin. I took three with another glass of water. "I had a wedding at the inn," I said. "Barry came by to make sure I had everything I needed—there had been a change in the number of guests we were expecting. He always did that—checked to make sure everything was okay, there was nothing I needed."

I stopped, and it was the man from the district attorney's office who prompted me. "And after that?"

I shrugged. "You probably already know that someone was here from ICE," I said. "He'd—interviewed me, I guess. Told me that Barry might have been running a scam out of the inn. I—I wanted to see if Barry was going to say anything. He must have known that

Ali—Agent Hakim—was talking to people. I thought he might bring it up." I hesitated. "Maybe tell me that it was all nonsense. But he didn't bring it up, and so I didn't, either. I chickened out."

"It seems like a coincidence," said Dennis Ramirez, "that he should get murdered on the same day that Immigration and Customs Enforcement happens to show up."

I frowned. "Are you stating a fact or looking for my opinion? Because I don't have one."

Julie said, "Sydney—"

"No," I interrupted her. "There's no reason to ask my opinion. I don't have an opinion. I don't even have a background in detection, though I *have* read a few Agatha Christies. And I've played Clue once or twice. But I don't think it was Professor Plum in the library with a candlestick this time." I stopped myself. "Sorry. But I'll be honest, I feel like shit, and I miss Barry." That was the reason I'd had so much to drink last night.

"You still don't seem surprised that we're investigating his death as a murder," said the man from the DA's office.

"Dennis—you don't mind if I call you Dennis, do you?—I'd have been surprised if it had been anything else. Barry hated water. There was no way that he would have been

117

anywhere near that pool if he didn't absolutely have to. So someone was there with him. And I can't think that anybody would have left him there to drown if that wasn't what they wanted to have happen."

"Except," said Dennis, "that he didn't drown."

I just stared at him. Some giddy overtired part of my brain was saying, see, it really *was* Professor Plum in the library with the candlestick. "What?"

He glanced at Julie, who hadn't moved, then came back to me, but didn't say anything. "There was no water in his lungs," Julie said.

So Ali *had* gotten everything fast-tracked. I felt a surge of gratitude. I'd call him, I promised myself. When the little men in my head with the anvils stopped. "So what killed him?" I asked.

It must have been my imagination, but it looked a lot like pity in her expression. "Poison," she said. "He was poisoned, Sydney."

***

I'd started drinking before I'd eaten anything: that was the problem. And after several hours spent in the sun, on the beach. A lethal combination.

I'd taken a quick shower when I got back from Herring Cove and then cycled down to the Lobster Pot, which looks like the world's biggest tourist trap but in fact has quite good food. I bypassed the dining room and climbed the stairs to the Top of the Pot, where I got a seat at the bar with a view of the harbor and thought about ordering a dozen oysters and instead ordered a mojito. Summertime drink.

And remembered sitting there with Barry, tequila shots with lime and salt, the whole silly drinker's ritual. His laugh, that great contagious laugh, laughing at me, at himself, at the world. Barry, who saw the humor in everything.

I ordered another mojito. Barry had a large bear claw tattooed behind his right shoulder. He was proud of his community—the community of Provincetown, the gay community, yeah; but the bear community was where his heart had been. Where he had been most completely himself. "Why?" I'd asked when I was first getting to know him. "What do you have in common, besides the way you look?"

He'd laughed. "Never underestimate how important looks are to a gay man."

I wasn't letting him get away with that. "But there's more. There's a lot more, isn't there?"

"Of course," he said. "Come on, another round."

"So tell me."

He signaled the bartender. "Okay," he said. "You know I was telling the truth about looks, right? How men all want other men based mostly on looks? Guys who work out, or guys who are all muscle. Not guys who are fat. Not guys like me." He paused as the bartender refilled our shot glasses and gave us more lemon wedges. "Cheers."

"Cheers."

He wiped his mouth with the back of his hand. "Imagine me, kid coming out, and there was no way you were getting me into a gym. Not ever. Got teased at school, I was always the pudgy kid. I didn't mean to be." He shook his head. "And I did enough physical work, I delivered groceries after school, worked in a lumber yard summers. I just never lost weight. And then, later…in the clubs…" A big sigh. "I wasn't the one getting picked up. I wasn't going home with anybody at the end of the night. Not when there were sleek slim hairless boys available." He picked up an additional wedge of lemon and sucked on it. "Funny thing was, I was growing into myself, and I was liking who I was. But I had to balance that with the fact that no one else seemed to."

"People are cruel," I said.

Barry shrugged. "Anyway," he said, "I started hearing about bear clubs. Hairy guys, big guys. Some of them overweight, some of them muscled—but it was all really accepting, you know? Something that the gay community was supposed to be, but wasn't."

I wanted to protest, but it wasn't my place. "So you became a bear."

"I did. I liked older men anyway, and they were the most accepting of all. It helped me, a lot. Having people around me who totally supported who I was, how I wanted to be in the world, that kind of thing." He shrugged. "Things change, of course. There's shallowness there too, don't get me wrong."

"As far as I can see," I said, "there's shallowness everywhere."

"Right on. But it's still the best people I've ever met. The place where I am accepted, where I can be myself." He looked at me. "My people."

I laughed. "You make it sound like a cult," I said.

He shook his head. "No coercion," he said. "You don't have to believe anything, or do anything. You can go to a bear gathering—like Bear Week here in P'town, or Bear Pride, or the International Bear Rendezvous—and just be yourself. For someone like me, that's priceless." He grinned. "I met Glenn at a Bear Pride march," he said.

The memory faded, and I found that while I was thinking about Barry I'd managed to order and consume two more mojitos. And someone had slid onto the barstool next to me, where I'd remembered Barry sitting. "Hey, Sydney."

I blinked blearily. "Hey, Mike." Just what I needed: another reminder. Or someone snapping at me, as I seemed to remember had been our last interaction.

He signaled the bartender and ordered a Sam Adams. "Whew. The place is a mess."

"What place?"

"Race Point Inn. Of course." He looked at me curiously. "You've been drinking."

I held up my glass. "And still am."

"So I see. Not sure I've ever seen you drinking, Sydney."

"It's an exciting sight," I said. "You've been missing something for sure."

"Uh-huh." He nodded his thanks to the bartender and took a long swig of beer. He'd apparently forgotten our little spat, which was nice, as I couldn't have possibly argued about anything.

"I miss Barry," I informed Mike. I'd gotten to the point where I was enunciating my words very carefully and feeling a minor triumph when they came out correctly. Or even semi-correctly. What the hell. "I miss him a lot."

He nodded. "Yeah," he agreed, surprisingly. "I keep expecting to look up and see him. And I was just walking down Commercial Street, could have sworn I saw him twice. Guys look like him." He took a swig of beer. "Guess it takes time to say good-bye." He paused. "Guess we should be talking about the funeral."

I nodded at the bartender. In for one mojito, in for four. "Don't have the body back yet," I said, and nodded wisely. "You need a body for a funeral," I informed him. "Besides, you know that Martin's all over it. All *over* it. He'll want to—conduct it. Like an orchestra." I nodded wisely; that felt like a brilliant analogy.

"Uh-huh," Mike said. "Sydney, how much have you been drinking?"

"A lot," I said as the mojito was put in front of me. I played with it, crushing the mint leaves with the straw. "A lot," I concluded.

I had a passing thought about interrogating Mike about Barry's secret lover, but I wasn't positive that I could manage the question. Articulating words seemed more and more difficult. We talked about something—

God only knows what—before Mike got up. "Come on," he said. "I'm taking you home."

"I'm fine."

"You're far from fine. Leave your bike, you can get it tomorrow. Let's go."

"I have to pay."

"You can pay me back," Mike said. "Come on, Sydney."

And that was how I'd wound up blinking blearily at Julie and the man from the district attorney's office. And vowing never to drink again.

Yeah. *That* could happen.

12

Julie and the guy from the DA's office hadn't been gone for very long when the phone rang. I winced and picked it up. "Sidney? It's Ali."

"Ali," I said. I wished he wouldn't shout.

"Are you okay?"

"Of course I'm okay." Whatever my issues were, I wasn't sharing them with ICE.

"All right," he said. "I wanted to let you know that I'll be there this afternoon."

"Where, there? Here? In P'town?"

He sounded amused. "Yeah, that there. I had a talk with my supervisor. And I still need to get some more information."

"Barry's dead," I said. "Whatever he did is over now."

"I know," he said, his voice unexpectedly gentle. "And I'm sorry, Sydney, but I can't close the investigation yet. But I want to keep you caught up with it."

"Okay." If he wanted to share, then that was something else altogether. "Do you want to have lunch?" I asked. *I might even feel halfway human by then.*

"Sure." He sounded surprised, and I wondered if I'd really been that prickly. Probably so.

One very long hot shower, three glasses of water, and five more aspirins later, I was dressed semi-respectably in a skirt and lace t-shirt, my hair more or less cooperating, and my sunglasses at the ready. I'd told Ali to meet me at Fanizzi's out in the East End, where there actually might be parking for his car, and he was waiting when I arrived. I was seriously impressed. He might be able to get out of a speeding ticket through the brotherhood of law enforcement, but anyone who could make any time on any road on the Cape during the season was either very good or very lucky.

"*Ecco. La bella signorina,*" Ali said as I approached. He was leaning against the Mustang and looked startlingly delectable.

I pushed the thought out of my head. I wasn't in the mood to delectate. "I thought you were Lebanese, not Italian."

"I am a man of many skills," he said.

I wasn't going to comment on that. I led the way into the restaurant, and we sat at a table against the window. The tide was high and the water was lapping the sand underneath us; Fanizzi's is built out over the high-tide mark. I sipped my water and looked out at the harbor. The day was clear and I had a good view of the Pilgrim Monument.

Beside me, suddenly, a gull screamed.

I jumped and spilled my drink. Ali reached across with his napkin, quick, efficient. "Sorry," I said, and "Here, let me help you," he was saying; and "No, no, it's all right," I said. We looked at each other and I realized, suddenly, how ridiculous I was being. I started laughing and Ali cracked a smile and then he was laughing, too.

"All right," I said finally. "I'm sorry I'm being such a bitch."

"It's okay," he said. "What you're going through is scary. And you're missing Mr. Parker."

"Yes," I said, waving aside the waiter with the cocktail menu. What I *didn't* need was more alcohol in my system. "And not knowing why—it's amazing how important that's

127

become. Like I could deal with it better if I knew why. That's stupid, isn't it? It won't bring him back. What I know or don't know—it doesn't matter."

"It does matter. The truth always matters. Yeah, maybe it doesn't matter now what Mr. Parker was or wasn't doing, and whether or not that came back to bite him—but it'll help you sleep at night. If you don't know, you'll always wonder."

"Here's what I wonder," I said, my worst fear surfacing. "If there were something I could have done. If I could have changed anything."

"You know what they say about suicides," said Ali, "that if they're really determined to do it, they're going to find a way, somehow, some day." I nodded. "The same is true of murder. If the only solution, the only way out of a situation, is to kill someone, then that's what's going to happen. And there's nothing that anyone can do to stop that."

We ordered sandwiches and I said, "So, tell me. Do you think it's coincidental that you came here to investigate Barry and he got killed one the day you arrived?"

He was looking out at the harbor. Someone had rented a sailboat from Flyer's and was approaching a fishing boat at anchor way too fast. Ali appeared fascinated. He brought his attention back to me reluctantly. "Province-town's been on our radar for a while," he said. "Not hard to see why. It's Wedding Central down here."

"I know," I said. "It's how I make my living, remember?"

"Right. And your inn's the only one that seems to be specializing in doing weddings," he said. "So we were going to look at Mr. Parker eventually, sooner rather than later. As for the timing…well, you know how on all the cop shows on TV, someone always says, 'I don't believe in coincidence'?"

Ali Hakim watched cop shows? I was fascinated. "Right," I agreed.

"I've never understood that," he said. The sandwiches arrived and he waited until the waiter was gone. "Of course there are coincidences in life. That's why we have a word for them." He shook his head. "In this case, though—well, it does seem to point to some questions."

"It points to a whole lot of questions," I agreed. "It seems to me that whoever killed Barry was fine until you were scheduled to show up. You'd made an appointment, right?"

"Right."

"So what about your investigation did this person not want to have happen? Was it something you were going to tell Barry? Or something Barry was going to tell you?"

He nodded. "Good questions."

"Or maybe," I continued, "it had nothing to do with you, and had something to do with Bear Week. Maybe the killer was in town for it, so this was the only time he could do it. Then it really would be a coincidence that you arrived then." I shook my head. "I don't know *how* to get answers to any of these questions, that's the problem. Are you listening?"

"I'm listening," he assured me. "You don't think the police will find the answers?"

"Of course they will!" My loyalty to Julie was unshakable. "But…"

"But you'd like to set your own mind at rest," he said. "You want to be careful, Sydney. Maybe leave the investigations to the investigators."

"You didn't even know him," I said, taking it for granted that he'd be doing some investigating himself.

"And maybe that helps," he said, his eyes straying back to the harbor where the Flyer's rental had somehow avoided collision and was weaving a quick if erratic path toward the channel where the ferries came in.

I am constantly amazed that people don't get killed out there.

13

I headed back to the inn after lunch. We might be acting out our own personal drama here, but weddings were fast approaching and it might be helpful for me to actually do my job instead of playing detective.

Jason was at the front desk. "Don't you ever go home?" I asked.

"Need the money, honey," he said. "Some of us can't go traipsing off to lunch at Fanizzi's whenever the spirit moves us."

"There are no secrets in this town," I said, turning the guest register around so I could look at it.

"None, thank goodness," he said. "*And* I hear that you were with Mr. Tall Dark and Handsome, to boot."

I glanced up. "Next you'll be telling me what we ordered."

"I wouldn't mind ordering *him*, honey! Oooh, ooh!"

"You said he's straight," I reminded him. I'm never sure. The fact that we'd been flirting was meaningless; I've had some of my best flirtations with gay men.

"Give me time," Jason said, reverting to his favorite topic. "I could change his mind."

"I'm sure you could." I swiveled the book back. "What kind of secret expensive habit do you have, anyway?"

"Sorry?"

"That keeps you glued to the reception desk." Two bears went by, laughing, and Jason waited until they were out of earshot. "I just like the scenery. You can't beat it."

"Uh-huh." I wasn't particularly listening; everyone in P'town needs money, and I'd just been making conversation. "Mike in his office?"

"Yes, dear, and take my word for it, you don't want to go there." He dropped his voice dramatically. "He's scared to death, Sydney, trying to find where that money went."

"I thought it was an accounting mistake."

"Well, of course it's an accounting mistake. And try finding another bookkeeper in the season! What a drama! But Glenn's definitely looking for answers, and we all have to mind our p's and q's now, don't we?"

"Do we?"

"Well, he's the new boss, isn't he?"

"I suppose so." It still wasn't anything I wanted to think about. Not yet, anyway.

"*De mortui* and all that," said Jason practically, "but whatever Barry was or wasn't, he's gone now."

"The king is dead, long live the king."

He sighed. "Well, honey, I miss him, too. Nobody more than me, I assure you. But we have to take care of ourselves, don't we? No one else is going to."

"You surprise me," I said. "I thought you were holding out for a sugar daddy."

"You gotta kiss a lot of frogs before that happens."

I smiled. "You're mixing your allegories. And, anyway, I thought it was a prince the frog turned into, not a sugar daddy."

"Honey, someday my prince will come, and I'll grab him and ride him all the way to condos in Palm Beach and Venice and Paris...you'll see! But in the meantime, all I can do is stand here and look gorgeous."

"Well," I said philosophically, "some-body's gotta do it." I squeezed past him on my way to my little alcove and my desk and my computer. During our inane chatter, a serious idea had made its way into my brain.

Wasn't all of this timing just a little too for-tuitous? ICE decides to investigate Barry and before they can, he's killed? Was there a nefar-ious connection there, someone who didn't want Barry talking to Ali? I sat thought about it for a minute and then pulled up my records. At home I'd looked at my list of upcoming weddings, but maybe I should have looked in the other direction.

Half an hour later I had it. Out of eighty-three weddings we'd planned, organized, or just plain hosted last year, twenty-nine had one spouse born outside of the country. Albania. Bulgaria. Greece. Kyrgyzstan. Ukraine. Ger-many.

Kyrgyzstan?

Places I didn't even know how to pro-nounce, or could have found on a map. I frowned. Twenty-nine out of eighty-three seemed like a high percentage.

I thought about it for another minute and then reached for the phone and called Vernon. Okay, so maybe Provincetown just got a high percentage of these weddings, anyway; a lot of countries were worse than the States had been pre-Obama. Hell, a lot of countries still imprisoned or killed you for being gay, never mind getting married.

But it didn't hurt to check. Vernon married a lot of people who didn't have their ceremony at Race Point Inn, people whose weddings I had nothing to do with, who wouldn't show up in my records. If this was a general trend, if there really were a lot of non-Americans marrying Americans, then his stats should be more or less the same as ours. "Hey, you keep records of all your weddings, don't you?"

"Of course I do, Missy-poo."

"Can you look at last year and tell me how many weddings you performed, and then how many of those were for people who weren't American? That is, I'm interested in weddings where one of the spouses was American and the other came here from abroad."

"What a strange question!"

"We're just doing a survey," I said vaguely. "I'd appreciate it."

"For you, my darling, anything." Yeah: for me and my future business. I shook my head. Maybe this whole thing was making me just a little cynical. "Thanks, Vernon. Um—and listen, can you do it now? Get it to me later today?"

An exaggerated sigh. "Yes, all right, Sydney, if you insist."

"I'm grateful," I assured him, and disconnected.

Now what? *Breathe,* I told myself. *Just breathe.*

***

I was still sitting there reminding myself to take in and discharge oxygen when my phone rang. "Sydney? I'm back!" The voice was high and excited.

I smiled; I couldn't help but smile. "Mirela!"

"Of course, and you have missed me!"

"Terribly," I admitted, though it hadn't been a question. Mirela took it for granted. And she was, of course, right. If she hadn't been in transit when all of this was happening, she'd have been the one I would have called.

Her voice was breathy. "And I have missed you terribly. I could not bring you back the hot springs, no, but I have pastries I smuggled through customs!"

All roads, it seemed, led back to the border. And to immigration. Mirela Petrovna had first come to Provincetown on an H2B visa, leaving her Bulgarian town behind so she could make serious American money for art school. She got a job in housekeeping at Race Point Inn, added in a few evenings a week carrying tourists around in a pedicab, and realized, in the midst of it all, that she'd happened upon the oldest continuously operating art colony in the United States and really didn't want to go back to Bulgaria after all. She commuted to the Museum School in Boston for a couple of years, briefly opened a vanity gallery in Wellfleet, and then joined the rather prestigious group of artists represented by the Beckett Gallery on Commercial Street. We had one of her paintings in reception; it had been a gift. Mirela's work was hard to afford, these days.

Her "road to citizenship," as it seemed to be called now, had been cleared by her talent, and she'd passed breezily through the green card stage and now carried an American passport. I'd wondered, at the time, about what it felt like, giving up your nationality. These days, with American borders closed and the Statue of Liberty weeping on her pedestal, I didn't wonder anymore. The huddled masses could keep yearning to breathe free as far as the current administration was concerned.

"Where are you?" I demanded now. I'd loved Barry and I loved Jason; but I considered Mirela a sister. Not a real one, because my real sister would have asked me what else I could have expected, living with all those gay people, but the sister I'd have liked to have instead.

"Boston," said Mirela. "I am staying here tonight. There is a reception." A pause. "You are not all right, I think, Sydney."

"No." I took in a breath. "I am very far from all right."

There was a pause, and I could hear the scrape of a match and the first inhale-exhale on her cigarette. The news that smoking causes cancer hadn't penetrated everywhere, and Mirela was pretty sure she could will illness away. For all I knew, she could. "What is it, sunshine?" I think *sunshine* is a form of endearment in Bulgarian; she's never gotten the sarcastic use of it in English.

"Barry's dead," I said. "Maybe killed."

"Yes," she said calmly.

"You knew? How did you know?"

"It is on Facebook," she said. "You know that I am always looking at Facebook. Jason is telling about it on Facebook."

I was going to have words with Jason. "There's an ICE agent snooping around."

"Please? What is this, snooping?"

"Investigating," I said. No; that didn't really capture how reptilian the whole thing felt. "Looking into things that are none of his business."

"Ah," she said. "And this snooping, it surprises you?"

"This snooping, it angers me," I said. I seem to always fall into Mirela's speech patterns.

"This anger, this is naïve," she said. "The ICE, they can do anything. They are more dangerous than anyone else." She should know, I thought.

I sniffed and changed tack. "Anyway, I wish you'd come home. The police are investigating. The district attorney is investigating. And Glenn says that Barry had another boyfriend."

Another inhale-exhale on the cigarette. "Yes," she said at length. "He did."

14

I had never seen so many flowers in one place at once. And, mind you, I've been to my fair share of funerals.

They poured into the inn; both florists in town were getting business off of Barry's death. He had been well liked, I thought, feeling maudlin. Jason was totally in his element, directing deliveries and delivering a running commentary both on arrangements and the individuals who's sent them. "Really, roses, what was she *thinking*?"

"It's the thought that counts," I said, automatically.

"It's the *expression* of the thought," he corrected me airily and then looked past me to yet another delivery. "Oh, good, come this way, that one will look simply stunning on the reception desk!"

It was all thoroughly disheartening.

Glenn was around, but like a ghost; you saw him out of the corner of your eye, but every time you turned around he'd disappeared. In many ways it seemed that the Race Point Inn was back to normal, open for business. Adrienne was making her usual overwrought concoctions in the kitchen; Martin was snootily seating people at tables according to his perception of their status; and I was completely demoralized.

"Well of course there was someone else," Mirela had said. "But he was going to end it."

"Who was going to end what? And who was it?"

"Barry was going to end the affair," she said. "You know that he loved Glenn, always and forever." That was one of Mirela's pet phrases: always and forever. I usually found it charming. Now it was irritating. "Who was it?"

"Well," she said, as one settling down for a good gossip might say, her tone confidential, "you know the couple who bought the Murchison place?"

"The Gropius house?" It was hard not to know about them. Provincetown is still by and large a town of gabled roofs and shingles, and the house designed and built by Walter Gropius in the 1960s for his friends Carl and Dorothea Murchison has always stood out as an oddity. The house is a two-level slab with walls of glass. It stood empty for a couple of decades after Carl Murchison's death, and weeds grew up the hillside on which it perched; there were rumors of lights being seen there on foggy nights. People still spoke of it as the Murchison place, even though they were long dead. Then it was purchased, and the new owner launched an ambitious restoration of the house and grounds, developing the property into nine subdivisions. The view was to die for, or so I'd been told.

"That's the one," she said. "They bought the house. A wealthy couple. They live in New York City."

That didn't tell me anything: most of the high-end real estate in town had been or was being bought up by couples from New York City. Especially now that Cape Air planned flights out of JFK. "So what?" I asked, impatient.

"So one of them works in the city," Mirela said. I could hear her puff on her cigarette. "An architect, I think. A student of Gropius'

142

and he paid a fortune for the place. I don't think he comes out here often; no one I know has ever seen him."

I didn't ask her how she knew. Mirela knows everything. Her art studio isn't far from the Wired Puppy, and while the coffee there is good, the gossip is better. "And?" I asked impatiently.

"And with him away, the house is very beautiful and very empty and lonely. All those views and no one to share them with."

"Mirela!"

"So Barry was there. Every time Barry was not at the inn, Barry was there. He wasn't very discreet, even: people saw his car coming and going."

"And staying overnight?"

"Who knows? People aren't that interested, you know."

"Of course they are."

"Well, all right, I will be fair. Not overnight. But sometimes late at night. It's hard not to notice, especially in the winter, they're the only lights you can see from the breakwater. So he was going up there for secret *rendezvous*."

I didn't say anything. This was all wrong. Barry was in love with Glenn. Barry had always been in love with Glenn. They both played around, of course, that was completely acceptable and almost expected; but their hearts belonged to each other. I couldn't fathom Barry in another relationship. "What's so special about this guy?" I asked, a little rhetorically. It wasn't money; it couldn't have been money. Both Barry and Glenn had enough to start their own third-world country.

"Eh, who knows?" She didn't sound particularly interested. "But I do know that it was a secret."

"Well, of course it was a secret. Glenn—"

"It had nothing to do with Glenn," she interrupted me. "There are politics involved. Serious politics."

"I don't understand. What politics?"

"Politics that would not survive knowing about the affair." I didn't say anything, and she added, impatiently, "You assume that this person was a man."

I was nonplussed. "Of course it was a man," I said. "Mirela, Barry's a bear! He's as gay as gay…"

"But the couple that bought the house, it is a man and a woman. He is an architect." She paused dramatically. "And she—she is Yasmina Edwards."

Stunned doesn't even come close. I swallowed. "That's wrong," I said stupidly. "Yasmina Edwards is a former senator. Yasmina Edwards is a *Republican* former senator."

"This is all true. *And* Yasmina Edwards," said Mirela, "was having an affair with Barry Parker."

Now as I stood at the inn I looked at the flowers pouring in, and as soon as Jason checked out the cards, I catalogued them in my mind. Would Yasmina even send anything? Would there be something special from she and her architect husband?

What was Barry doing with a *woman*? The more I learned, the less sense it was making. I turned to Jason. "Hey, tell me something."

"Of course."

"Did you ever want to—you know—have sex with a woman? Like, as an experiment?"

"Darling, if you're coming on to me, you're doing it very tactlessly. Ooooh, look, something from that handsome man who runs the boatyard! Lilies, how perfect!"

"Jason," I said, "I'm serious. Did you ever want to try it? Just to see?"

He looked at me. "You *are* serious. Good heavens. Sydney, darling, no, no, a thousand times no. You know that I adore you, but going to bed with a woman?" He gave a little moue of distaste. "I feel a *frisson* just *thinking* about it! Please. Mary Jane Tennant and I played show-me-yours-and-I'll-show-you-mine when I was five, and I've never seen one of them since. Never cared to."

"That's what I thought," I said.

"Why? Are you trying to convert someone? Because, poppet, please, don't. By the time someone figures out he's gay, believe me he's had enough pressure to be straight to know who he really is. It's not the easy route, but it's the right one."

I nodded. People didn't change like that. There was something else going on. There had to be something else going on.

One thing was clear: I'd chosen the right career path for myself. As an investigator, I was an abject failure.

***

Money.

It came to me just as I was drifting off to sleep: money. One of the TV crime dramas that I watch—or maybe all of them, I'm not above watching more than one, I'll admit it—once noted that people generally are killed by other people because of love, lust, or lucre. And lucre was money.

I sat up in bed and clicked on the bedside lamp. Ibsen raised his head, blinking a little. A steady bass line throbbed through the floor from the club downstairs.

I wasn't going near the love/lust thing: that still felt too much like a betrayal. But money. If Barry was making all this fantastic loot off his green-card business, where was it going?

"There's no money," I said to Ibsen. He yawned. Never a cat for details.

What I meant, of course, was not that there was no money at the inn; there was plenty of money at the inn. Barry had bought the place a long time ago and had taken out loans: a mortgage, a business loan, all that. He'd made a lot of money since, of course, and Glenn was in Key West because he'd been able to retire at the ripe age of forty-five after a career doing something on Wall Street; I was fuzzy on the details. Anyway, they were both very well off.

What I meant was I didn't see any influx of extra cash. Barry was fiscally conservative and got out of debt as quickly as he could; hell, he paid off his credit cards at the end of every month, something I've never managed. He'd driven the same car since I'd known him—a nice car, mind, a Mercedes, but nothing that required secret money. In the off-season he went down to Key West a bunch of times, but he lived with Glenn down there. They usually took one trip a year together, last year it was a nature tour of the Galapagos. Something I could only dream of, but well within their means.

Jason had talked about an expansion of the inn, but Barry didn't need illegal cash for that—if anything, that's the opposite that a thriving business needs, accounting that doesn't add up. He'd just use some of the inn's equity—which had to be formidable by now—to get a loan.

Illegal money coming in and now, it seemed, money disappearing from the inn as well. They had to be related. Didn't they?

"I'll find out tomorrow," I told Ibsen. He seemed fine with that.

15

I called my police contact first thing. "Well?"

"Well, what?" Julie demanded

I sighed. This was no time for her to turn all officious on me. "Well, did the tox screen come back?" I was betting that it had. I was betting that Ali's sister had quite a lot of pull. Julie had worked for the Boston Police Department before coming to Provincetown; hell, she might even have worked for Commissioner Hakim, or whatever the sister's name might be.

"You can buy me breakfast," said Julie, and disconnected.

She hadn't said where; she hadn't had to. All the year-rounders know that breakfast means Chach's over on Shank Painter Road, the closest thing that Provincetown has to a diner, and the most affordable food around. Tasty and plentiful dishes, and it's another place where, if you sat there long enough, you'd end up seeing everyone in town that you knew.

I hurried through my morning routine, combing my hair while brushing my teeth, the kind of multitasking that gives multitasking a bad name. Shirt, skirt, flats, and I was ready to go. There's always a line at Chach's—well, okay, there's always a line anywhere in the summertime—and I wanted to snag a table as quickly as I could.

I parked my bike and wedged myself between two groups of bears (trust them to find the best breakfast place around), waiting for Julie to arrive. I processed snippets of conversations while wishing I'd had the sense to grab a newspaper on my way over. "I saw him in Aspen. He didn't look well, he'd lost a lot of weight..." "So my partner's got his real estate license. Good for him. I wouldn't be able to stand that much time soothing ruffled feathers over the telephone..." "Have you been to the Portuguese bakery? Those bear-claw pastries..."

Chach's knows Julie, and a booth opened up soon after she arrived. Nice to carry some weight. "I want to find out what happened," I told her at once.

"I want to decide what to eat," she said, opening her menu.

"So," I said as soon as we'd ordered. "The tox screen."

Julie sighed and looked out the window next to us. "Someone administered ethylene glycol to Barry sometime in the afternoon," she said. "He probably reacted to it by feeling drunk and dizzy for a while. Probably not something he would have noticed." A quick glance at me and then away. "Later on, and into the night, he'll have gotten sick. It's painful." A deep breath. "Eventually he probably went into a coma. I hope so, anyway."

"What the hell is ethylene glycol?"

"It's one of the ingredients in antifreeze."

"Antifreeze?" I thought about it for a moment as the waiter filled our coffee cups. When he left, I said, "How do you get someone to drink antifreeze?"

Julie was stirring sugar into her cup. "It tastes sweet," she said. "You can put it in anything that's supposed to be sweet, even this," and she flicked the side of her cup with a fingernail. "Tea, coffee, soft drinks, whatever. All it does is make them taste sweeter."

"And you can just get this stuff anywhere? Anyone can go down to the hardware store and stock up on nails, two-by-fours, and poison?"

She nodded. "There are some states that mandate something non-toxic to be used in antifreeze instead," she said, "but Massachusetts isn't one of them."

I drank my coffee and thought about it. "When you first said poison," I said, "I thought that must narrow it down to someone who could get—oh, you know, stuff like arsenic or strychnine or something like that. I mean, if I wanted to poison somebody, I wouldn't have the faintest idea where to get it. But anyone can get antifreeze. It was on sale last week in Orleans."

"There's been some media attention around it from time to time," Julie said. "Mostly spouses killing each other for the life insurance. And every time it happens, there are a bunch of copycat killings, too. None in Massachusetts that I know of, though."

"It seems exotic."

"Antifreeze? Exotic?" She laughed. "I suppose so. It's not obvious, anyway. And Barry liked sweet drinks."

"He was a bear," I said and nodded.

"Exactly. Mojitos and margaritas."

"And Tom Collinses when he was feeling nostalgic," I added, feeling a little nostalgic myself. "How much of this stuff would it have taken? I mean, Barry was a big man."

"Relatively little, actually. And administered over the course of an afternoon and evening…" Her voice trailed off as our breakfasts were delivered. After we'd straightened out the questions of ketchup and more coffee and were alone again, she said, "So we know he was drinking. There was a party."

I nodded. "Some bear thing," I said. "They called it the Bear Necessities party."

"Right. And that means it will be okay, Sydney. This is straightforward police work. We're tracking down who was there, all day, from the afternoon on. Who was drinking with him. Who was serving, waiters, bartenders, everybody. Who was there before the party, who was there at the party, who stayed late. What time people arrived and what time they left. All that. We'll get a list and we'll go down the list, and we'll find out who did it. We're narrowing it down. We'll get there."

She sounded confident, and I had to admit that it seemed hopeful. At the very least it was something concrete, better than the questions and impressions that were swirling around in my head. But there was one issue I had to ask her about. "I still don't understand *why* anyone would want to kill him, Julie," I said, and there were abrupt tears in my eyes again. "I know there was a lot going on in his life, things I didn't know about. I'm pretty convinced by now that he was brokering green cards through the wedding service, and apparently there had been some threats there—you know about that, right?"

She nodded and swallowed a bite of egg. "We've been liaising with Agent Hakim."

I didn't want to talk about Agent Hakim, much less the unfortunate verbing of the word liaison. "And he was supposed to be seeing someone else, someone besides Glenn," I said.

She stared. "You think *Glenn* had something to do with this?"

"God, no," I said. But that was the problem: I couldn't imagine anyone I knew having anything to do with this. "I'm just adding things up. Maybe whomever he was seeing didn't want to share him with Glenn anymore." I was avoiding the word *woman*. "And Jason says that there've been heated arguments over Barry adding another floor to the inn."

"There are always heated arguments over any construction in this town."

"Well, yeah. But I'm reaching here. I still don't get anyone hating him enough to kill him." There was a long silence, and then I asked, in the smallest voice I've ever heard come out of myself, "Did he suffer a lot, Julie?" I was remembering his face, the expression on his face. It hadn't been peaceful.

"Yes," Julie said, watching me. "It was painful. It was good that he passed out."

I pushed my plate away. I couldn't eat anymore. I was seeing the face. I was thinking of what it would take someone to do that to another human being. *Breathe, Riley, just breathe.* "How can anyone hate that much?"

She was still eating; Julie's seen more death than I have. Not that that's saying much. "You're assigning normal human emotions to this person," she said briskly. "That's not how they think. That's not who they are. You don't have to hate someone to kill them. In fact, that's probably way down on the list of reasons. You just have to think that your life and your needs and everything about you is more important than their life, or their needs, or them—as a person." She sighed. "Look. Some of these other cases I was talking about? *Most* of these other cases I was talking about? It's husbands killing wives or wives killing husbands. You think they all hated each other? Bullshit. The person who got killed was inconveniencing their precious little lives. The person they killed was standing between them and financial ease, or a different spouse, or whatever it was that they wanted. They were so self-absorbed that everything was about them and that justified doing whatever they could to be happy."

I shivered. "How do they sleep at night?"

"You think it *bothers* them? Not for a second." She ate a bite of English muffin, swallowed, took a sip of coffee, put the cup down. "Listen, Sydney. Most of us think the same way. We follow rules that we all more or less agree make sense. That's how society works. And I'm here, law enforcement's here, in case someone *doesn't* follow the rules. But most of the time, people who don't follow the rules, it's because they think they're better than the rest of us, or different from the rest of us. They're above all that. So whatever they want, they feel justified in getting. They steal stuff. They text when driving. They kill somebody. Because everyone else is just a backdrop to their lives. We're the bit players; they're the stars. Why should they lose sleep? They got what they wanted."

"That's a dark view of the world," I said.

"Um, you *do* remember what I do for a living, right?" She shrugged. "Like I said, most people aren't like that. It's what keeps me going, that I'm taking care of the ninety-nine percent who *aren't* sociopaths."

I was pursuing my own line of thought. "But if someone's that self-centered, wouldn't it show?" I asked. "If you really don't care about anybody but yourself, then people would notice that, wouldn't they? I haven't seen anyone who acts like that around here."

"They're here, all right," she said darkly. "But most of them don't actually go so far as to kill. And also—well, at some level, they *know*. They know that they're not like everybody else. And they know that they have to blend in. So they develop adaptive behavior."

"You mean they act like actual human beings."

She smiled. "You could put it that way. It would be really unusual if you could spot a true sociopath in daily life. Not unless you were intimately involved with them." She shrugged. "Most of them pass, Sydney. But when we find this guy, you'll see. He'll start whining about how unfair it all is. Because he'll only be able to see life as it relates to him." She put her napkin to her lips. "And now I have to go see if I can do it," she said.

"Do what?"

"Catch him." She slid out of the booth. "Thanks for breakfast, Sydney."

I sat staring at the eggs congealing on my plate. Whatevers, as Jason would say: Julie was an expert, but I was still with my original thought: that it must take a lot of hatred to do that to somebody.

The waiter was hovering. "Will there be anything else?"

I dashed away the tears. "No. No, thank you." I got out my wallet. *Breathe, Riley.* It was still Bear Week, and there were weddings to organize.

Along with a funeral.

***

I drove to the municipal parking lot and was just getting out of the car when my mother called. Her timing is invariably perfect. "I was wondering," she said acidly, "if you were still alive, since you haven't called."

Not a great choice of words, under the circumstances. I sighed. "I'm busy, Ma. We're in the middle of the season."

"Don't try to make that absurdity sound like a débutante's ball."

Oh, right. Because there's *nothing* absurd about a débutante's ball. I juggled the phone, my purse, and the box of doughnuts I'd picked up at Stop & Shop while struggling out of the Little Green Car. I locked it, then looked around in my daily delusion that today would be the day I didn't lose my Honda in the sea of cars around me. "Did you want something?" I asked my mother.

"Is it too much to ask to hear your voice once in a while? Do I have to want something?"

Stand back, and watch an expert at work. My mother is seriously good at this. She invariably leads with an attack. Already in three sentences she'd let me know that I'd failed her, that I should be groveling, and that I shouldn't live in P'town. A maximum of manipulation in a minimum of time. The woman's got skills.

"I'm at work," I said. It's never deterred her before, but hope springs eternal and all that. I was walking as briskly as anyone can walk in P'town in the summer. If I played my cards right, I'd lose the cell signal.

No such luck. "Your father was wondering if you're going to make it for his birthday," she said.

My father's birthday is in October. "Ma," I said despairingly.

"*And* he said that Ralph Henderson is back in town. He saw him this morning at the hardware store!" She sounded triumphant.

Ralph Henderson is the CEO of a moderate-sized company and is shockingly (to my mother's mind, anyway) still single.

"Good for him," I said. As I wobbled by I waved at an acquaintance hanging out in front of the Coffee Pot in Lopes Square.

"We thought you could come to dinner on Sunday," my mother continued, and added, as though presenting the ultimate inducement, "We're having that chicken dish you like. You know, the one your cousin made up."

The chicken dish my cousin made up is heavily dependent on Campbell's cream of mushroom soup for flavor. A gourmet's dream. "What is it," I demanded, "that you don't understand about it being the season here? You know? The summer season? Tourists? Weddings?"

"Always someone else's wedding," she said darkly, and then went on as if I hadn't said anything, "We were going to invite Ralph Henderson on Sunday, too. Wouldn't that be nice?"

"Go ahead," I said. I scooted around a group of bears trying to determine where to go for lunch. "Invite Ralph Henderson. He might be up for the chicken dish. I don't have time for it."

"You'll never catch a husband like that." Her voice was sepulchral.

"I don't want a husband, Ma," I said. What I really wanted was a vacation. July is way too early in the Silly Season to be thinking about a

160

vacation. I got to the inn, hopped up the steps, then turned and sat down on the top one. This was one conversation I didn't need Jason overhearing. "I already had a husband once, remember?"

"Just because you failed that time doesn't mean that someone like Ralph Henderson wouldn't be willing to take you on. You could do it better, this time."

Take me on? I blinked. "Ma, I'm at work," I said. "I have to go."

"So what did you decide about Sunday?"

"The same thing I said when you first brought it up. I can't leave the Cape." Hell, I couldn't leave *Provincetown*, much less the Cape, and that was when my boss *hadn't* been murdered. "I'm going to hang up now."

"No wonder you are so bad at relationships," my mother said. "I've never taught you anything, like not hanging up on people?"

Breathe, Riley. Just breathe. "Good-bye, Ma," I said, and disconnected before she could say anything else. Almost instantly a text message announced itself. "We'll set a place for you on Sunday."

The only thing more puzzling than why someone had killed Barry was why someone *hadn't* killed my mother.

16

Glenn was sitting in the bar area off reception, alone, flipping halfheartedly through the *Banner*, a half-drunk cup of coffee sitting on the bar. I hoisted myself onto the stool next to him and touched his shoulder lightly. "How you doing?"

He looked up from the newspaper. "Hey, Sydney," he said. "I'm okay."

He didn't look okay. He looked like he hadn't slept in about a month. Even by bear standards, he needed a shave. And you could have packed for a weekend away in the pouches under his eyes. A long weekend. "What's happening?" I asked.

A shrug, and he picked up his coffee, tasted it, made a face and set it down again. "Julie says they'll release the—release Barry tomorrow," he said.

"That's good news, right?" Even to my own ears, I sounded just a tad too hearty.

"I suppose it is," he said. He looked at me. "Did she tell you?"

"About…?" I knew damn well about what, but I wasn't going to be the first one to use the word antifreeze.

He sighed and shook his head, letting the question go. "I should have been here."

"It wouldn't have made a difference," I said quickly. "Don't do that to yourself, Glenn. You couldn't have done anything even if you'd been here. Whatever—whoever did this, you weren't going to keep them from doing it." I was really hoping what I was saying was true. If Glenn had been here, then someone probably wouldn't have been able to doctor Barry's drinks all afternoon and all night, not without being noticed. But maybe Ali was right, and there wasn't anything that would have stopped the killer. If this hadn't worked, chances are he'd have found some other way to do it.

Glenn didn't say anything, and I took a deep breath. "You must know some of the guys who were at the bear party," I said. It's like a circuit: there's a bear event in San Francisco, and then one in Miami, and then one in P'town, and round and round they went. There were newcomers, of course, and older guys dropping out, moving on, but there was a core constituency, too. Men who had known each other for years, who saw each other at all the events, who could be counted on to show up. Hell, I wasn't into bear culture, and yet for the past four days even I'd been seeing familiar faces, hearing voices I remembered, greeting guys whose names I could recall without too much effort. Glenn had to have known at least half the guys hanging out around the pool that afternoon, partying into the evening.

He put down the newspaper. "I knew most of them. So what?" he asked quietly. "What do you want me to do, Sydney? Try to imagine which one of my friends wanted my partner dead?"

Ouch. Put it that way, and I was nothing more than a nosy busybody. "Oh, God, Glenn, I'm sorry," I said. "I wasn't thinking…"

"I know," he said, shaking his head. "It's all right. Believe me, I've been asking myself the same question. Just felt—uncomfortable, hearing you say it out loud."

I nodded. "Like saying it makes it more real," I said and, unbidden, a line from a ceremony I'd listened to that spring came into my head: "Why do we speak our vows?" asked the woman officiant. "Because, for many of us, language makes the abstract become real. Speaking them means standing behind them."

Like speaking the name means putting a face to the killer.

Glenn sighed. "I just think of all of them," he said, "you know? Guys I've been friends with for over a decade, people we've traveled with, gotten drunk with, hell, even gone camping with, if you can picture that. I've sat with some of these guys when they got bad diagnoses, and when they broke up with their partners, and when they came out to their workplaces. And now I have to think about them all, one by one, and wonder which one wanted Barry dead. Wanted him to suffer."

I wasn't so sure about that last bit. I thought that probably the suffering part wasn't the main goal; it was probably a side effect of the availability of the antifreeze. But I could have been wrong, and I also certainly didn't think it would help to say any of that to Glenn. Time to change the subject. "Is there anything I can do?" I asked. "Anything I can help with? Take something off of your plate?"

He shrugged. "I don't even know," he said. "That's the absurdity of it all. I don't know. Barry and Mike have been running the place between them, and I've been out of the loop for a while. Intentionally. Too many cooks, and all that...plus, I wanted to focus on the bar."

"Your place in Key West," I said, nodding.

"Yeah, guess it's all mine now, isn't it?" He shook his head. "There's too much. It would have been hard enough if it had been a normal thing, Barry having a heart attack or something like that, but this? Feels like everything's put on hold until we know."

"I get that," I agreed. "But seriously, Glenn, you could probably help Julie. If you don't want to think about the person who did it, maybe you can narrow down *why* they did it." I saw his face and added, quickly, "I know you don't want to know if it's a friend. But we have to find out, and you know Julie will, sooner or later. It'll go to court, somewhere, somehow it'll go to court. Even if it's a friend. But he still killed Barry, Glenn. Isn't it worth figuring it out for Barry?"

"Figuring it out is going to help Barry?"

"Yes!" I caught myself and lowered my voice. "You have to know all the things that people are saying. About him running an illegal business out of the inn. About the money missing from the accounts. About the condo owners next door. Yeah, not everybody knows all of that yet, but you know this is a small town. Probably no one will say anything on the Provincetown Community Space page on Facebook, but they'll talk about it, you know they will. Ptown's a bunch of old biddies gossiping half the time. I don't want them gossiping about Barry!"

"They will anyway."

"And you'll sit here and you won't do anything about it." I slid off the barstool. "To hell with that, Glenn."

I'd already started for the door when he said, "I think it has something to do with the Murchison place."

That stopped me, all right. I turned around. "What do you know about the Murchison place?"

"Probably the same thing that you know," he said. "That Barry was spending a lot of time up there."

"I don't see when," I said. "It seems that he was always here. And," I added as he started to say something, "he never brought anyone here, Glenn. Cross my heart."

"I believe you. But I know he was there a lot."

"How?"

"What?" He sounded genuinely puzzled.

"How did you know?"

He looked away. "Jason told me."

"Jason?" What the hell did he have to do with this? "How would Jason know?"

Glenn was looking everywhere but at me. "He followed him."

"He *followed* him?"

"If you're just going to repeat everything I say, this conversation isn't going anywhere," he said irritably, folding his newspaper. "And don't ask me why. Jason has his own way of looking at the universe."

"Yeah," I said. "With him at the center." I was going to have some words with Jason. Once he told me what he knew, of course.

"All right, so his motives weren't pure," said Glenn. "But the fact remains that he followed Barry there. Often, he said." He shook his head. "I'd been thinking that Barry was seeing someone else, you know? That he was, like, maybe in love with someone else. But he's been going up to the Murchison place for a long time, Jason says, over a year, and only the Gropius house has anybody in it during the winter. And it's a straight couple that lives there. So something else is going on."

Well, it was a far better hypothesis than that of Barry having fallen for a woman, I had to admit. And maybe whatever was happening up there was the answer to where the extra money from the green card scam was going, too. That one was still baffling me.

It was all actually quite comforting.

"What we need to do," I said to Glenn, "is go up there ourselves and see."

He stared at me. "You can't be serious."

"Of course I can be serious. I'm being serious right now. If the answers are up at the Murchison place, then that's where we need to go."

"And say what, exactly? Did you have something to do with Barry Parker's death?" He looked like he was about to cry again.

"Exactly," I said. "Oh, Glenn, won't it make you feel better? To know?" I took a deep breath. "And not just you: all of us. Barry's friends. And the inn...well, I don't know what your plans are for this place, but rumor and innuendo won't help it on Trip Advisor."

"There's no rumor and innuendo."

Were we back to that? "Glenn," I said in exasperation, "Julie will get to the bottom of all this, but she'll do it a lot faster if we help her. And she has to follow the legalities. She probably needs a search warrant, or something like that. Whereas we..."

"...can trespass to our little hearts' delight," Said Glenn. "All right, you've made your point. Tomorrow."

"Why not right now?"

"Because right now," he said heavily, "I have to go over to Gately's and pick out a coffin."

There didn't seem to be anything adequate I could say to that, so I kept my mouth shut.

It was time to check in with Jason, anyway. He was at the front desk. It was hard to believe he'd found time to shadow Barry, since he seemed to be always at the front desk. "What is this," I said, coming straight to the point, "about you following Barry around?"

"And hello to you, too," he said tartly. He was staring at his phone again. I grabbed it away from him in exasperation. "Hey!" he protested.

"That can wait," I said, glancing down at the screen. He was on Zillow. Better, perhaps, than Grindr, which might have scared me to death. "I want to know why you've been following Barry, and why you told Glenn and not me. You two aren't exactly buddies."

He gave a mock shiver. "Heaven forbid!"

"So?"

"Well, honey, I told you before. How irritating that you don't remember our conversations from one day to the next. It doesn't *do* to not get in good with the new boss, does it?"

"What, you've been following Barry around for a year just in case someone were to murder him so you could ingratiate yourself with his bereaved partner? *That's* the story you want me to believe?"

He gave an exaggerated sigh and reached out a hand for his phone. "No, if you really want to know, I just was super-curious, and as I have no life whatsoever in the winter, I thought I'd do a bit of sleuthing."

I held on to the phone. I was getting *déjà vu* from my conversation with Mirela. "He went to the Murchison estate? Every time? How often?"

"Every time, honey, twice a week with tedious regularity."

"How'd he get in?"

"What do you mean?"

"I mean," I said impatiently, "that there's a tremendous iron gate at the entrance. That's locked. And before you tell me that there are gaps in the fence, I'll tell you that I've become ready to believe certain things about Barry, but not that he was keeping midnight assignations by crawling up the hill through the underbrush in winter. That's asking a little too much."

"Of course he didn't. Don't be ridiculous. He had a key. *Now* can I have my phone back?"

I gave him his phone back.

I thought about checking in with Julie. I thought about actually doing my job and making some phone calls to arrange details about a whole slew of weddings that were scheduled to take place, murder or no murder, over the next three weeks. I thought about calling Mirela and telling her to get her butt home so she could pick up some more gossip. I thought about telling my mother I had a terminal allergy to matrimony. I thought about Ali Hakim's eyes.

And, finally, I gave it all up and went home.

***

I tried reading and watching Netflix and doing my nails and my brain couldn't settle on anything. Finally, more out of desperation than a real thought that I'd get anywhere, I looked up the Murchison estate online.

Designed by pioneering Bauhaus architect Walter Gropius (and one of few residential projects he took on) and other designers from The Architects Collaborative, known for its sophisticated aesthetic of simplicity and purity of line, this project used a Japanese temple as its central inspiration: there are two roofs with a clerestory of glass between them, flooding the interior with light and using the crest of the hilltop site to give access to the outdoors from each room.

Principal rooms are on the upper level to take advantage of the seaside views. The lower floor contains functional rooms such as an office and guest accommodations. A change in ground level at the front of the house links the motor court with the front entrance and the garage. Landscaping includes a terrace that spans three sides of the house and widens into a big terrace designed for dancing. This joins a 25-ft by 50-ft swimming pool and two small cabanas, each with dressing rooms and laundry facilities for guests. The surrounding plantings of Ink trees, Bayberry bushes and Dwarf Pines are placed informally to soften the horizontal lines of the façade, and mature along with the house.

All the fabrics, carpets, lighting fixtures and furniture were custom-designed by the architects to fit its original occupants. Major rooms are banded with a lighting frieze of vertical walnut strips and plastic placed below the clerestory windows.

Well, okay. That was interesting. But then I came to the part of the story that I remembered, the part that had been a raging local controversy when I first moved to town.

Schorer's $6.55 million purchase of the 3.5-acre parcel, formerly owned by Barbara Murchison, got off to a rocky start in 2008. The development plan became embroiled in a dispute between several town boards and Schorer over his proposal to build new homes on a piece of property that had become iconic in Provincetown for its main house, designed by famed architect Walter Gropius, and its sweeping views of the harbor, moors and West End breakwater.

It had been before my time in Provincetown, but it was coming back to me now; now the events seemed a tempest in a teapot, though at the time apparently passions were running high in a conflict between the town and the developer over dividing up the property and adding more modern houses that "didn't fit in" according to some vocal opponents—though how they thought the Gropius house "fit in" was a bit of a stretch.

But the controversy had settled, the houses had been built—one of them by two architects rivaling Gropius himself in fame and prestige—and though we still called it the "Murchison place," not a lot of people, these days, had known it back when the controversial psychologist and his wife had lived there.

And now another architect lived there. With *his* wife. Some of the time. The puzzle of Barry's visits to the estate wasn't any clearer than it had been when I started.

I still couldn't believe that he was seeing anyone other than Glenn, and I certainly couldn't believe that he had rebelled against nature enough to be seeing a woman. It was as impossible as anything that relates to human behavior could be.

Not that I was any expert. As my mother drearily and repetitively pointed out, I hadn't been all that good at marriage myself.

17

Ibsen didn't even look up when I left the next morning. He was getting used to living alone again. It happens every summer, and every summer he goes through the dramatics attached to my leaving...well, for the first few days, anyway. After that he settles into his routine, which, as far as I can ascertain, involves marathon sessions of sleep so that he'll be rested enough to tear madly about the place at three in the morning.

He times it well. The last Lady Gaga piece shakes the building at two o'clock, when the club closes, and by three I'm in the deepest sleep I ever get in the season. Just in time to have a cat fling himself onto my stomach.

Some winter day I'm staying in all day and clanging pots by his head to keep him awake all day. So there.

Mirela was arriving at noon—thank goodness—but I had a wedding in the meantime. And as it was actually the way I made a living, it might be good to pay attention to it.

Jason was, inevitably, at the desk. "Sydney, darling!" he exclaimed. "Only the best wedding organizer in P'town!"

"What do you want?" I asked.

He pouted. "Why do I have to want anything?"

"Because you generally do," I said, then relented. "Never mind. You doing okay?"

"Only since you walked in to brighten my drab *prêt-à-porter* day," he said. "Seriously, Sydney, it's enough to lose your mind. There was no one I even wanted to dance with at the Vault last night. *Quelle crise!* My life is too sad for words."

"I expect you'll make up for it tonight," I said vaguely, sorting through the mail from my cubbyhole. "What do you imagine the Lighthouse Trust wants with me?"

"I imagine," he said austerely, "they want you to give them money."

"Ha. They must have confused me with someone who stays at Race Point, not someone who works here. When are my brides arriving?"

He consulted his book. "Checked in last night," he said. "They should be in the spa as we speak, getting all relaxed for the ceremony."

"That's fine, then." I'd have chosen the spa for getting relaxed afterward, though maybe the champagne would do that. Like I said, I wasn't devastatingly proficient at the whole wedding/marriage thing myself, so what did I know? "You ever think of getting married?" I asked Jason.

"My dear, if that's a proposal, you could at least taken a knee first."

"I can't marry you," I said. "You're allergic to cats."

"I am devastated," said Jason with all the seriousness and dignity that he could muster, "to learn that you'd put that wretched animal before me, your nearest and dearest."

"Yep. And your devastation will only last until the next pretty boy strolls in."

"What can I say?" he asked rhetorically. "I'm shallow, everyone knows that."

"And there you are," I said, shoving all my mail back into the cubbyhole. "That's why I stick with Ibsen."

"Because I'm shallow?"

"Because he's inscrutable. Do you know where Glenn is?"

"Oh, lordy, he got in just a few minutes before you did. Poor man. Probably getting coffee."

"He was out early," I said, hinting. If Jason didn't know it, it wasn't worth knowing.

"Darling, it's too *too* tragic. He was at Gately's."

"Oh." The light bantering mood came crashing down. There's never anything good you can say to or about someone who's just been to a funeral home. "I'm off, then. And just in time. Unless I'm wrong, those are not one but two pretty boys coming this way."

"You're not wrong," Jason said, eyes sparkling, somehow just managing to not actually push me out of his way, his gaze firmly on the door. Without looking around, he added, "Don't you have somewhere to be?"

"I'm going, I'm going." I could use a coffee myself, come to think of it. Behind me, I could hear Jason greeting the new arrivals. "Well, *hello* there, handsome men!"

As I made my way to the dining room I could still hear their voices behind me.

Glenn was indeed having coffee, sitting on one of the tapestry-covered loveseats (which, it has to be said, he completely dwarfed), drinking coffee and staring at pretty much nothing. I helped myself from the samovar and took a seat in the easy chair at right angles to the loveseat. "Hey, Glenn."

He glanced at me briefly then his gaze moved away again. His eyes were rimmed with red. "Sydney."

"What's going on?" I asked carefully. From where I was sitting, there wasn't anything going on. At least in Glenn's head.

"They're releasing the—they're releasing Barry," he said, his voice flat. He ran his tongue over his lips. "I've been sending out invitations and announcements for the funeral," he said.

Wow. Nothing much that anyone could say to that, right? I tried anyway. "I'm so sorry, Glenn."

He nodded. He had that thousand-yard stare going on again. I reached over and took his hand and gave it a shake. "There will be lots of people there," I promised. "Everybody loved Barry."

Okay, nice, Riley. Open mouth, insert foot.

Glenn didn't even bother pointing out the obvious, that there was at least one person who didn't love Barry. "Most of our friends are staying through Saturday, for the funeral," he said. It might not sound like it, but that was actually a big deal. Some of the bears had arrived on Saturday, so it would be easy for them to attend a funeral on the following Saturday, pack, and leave. But some of them would have arrived on Friday, and staying the extra day involved expense and hassle: an extra night's fees, and the probability that they wouldn't be able to stay at the same inn, which would have booked their rooms for the following week. They must really, really have loved Barry.

It was all very touching and, at the same time, very melancholy. Because having all those people who loved him didn't keep the one person who didn't from killing him. Someone must have really hated him…

Okay, I know, Julie gave me that introduction to sociopaths at Chach's; she'd said that hatred didn't necessarily have anything to do with it. But I was still stuck there. You *had* to hate someone to continuously ply them with a poison that you knew would bring on a painful and prolonged death. I sighed. This was all too complicated; I felt like my brain was getting twisted.

"I have a wedding," I said at length, as Glenn showed no interest in prolonging the conversation. "We're still going up to the Murchison place this afternoon, right?"

He focused on me. "Yeah. Sure."

"Okay," I said.

I grabbed my coffee and headed out. When I glanced back, Glenn was still staring into space.

***

The wedding was scheduled for 11:00, and I had the patio area ready by 10:30. Somewhere in the inn I could imagine my two brides getting ready, giggling together, savoring every moment of this perfect day. They had never met Barry. Their day had no bear-shaped shadows case across it.

The officiant and photographer arrived together, laughing about something. I was just settling the champagne bottle into the ice bucket, and Gregg—the photographer—was already taking pictures of it. "I'm off," he announced; the brides had no doubt asked for some photos in their room.

The officiant was buttoning up her cassock. "Are you okay?" she asked.

I looked up, startled. "Not really," I said and swallowed. "The funeral's tomorrow."

She nodded, clasping her leather folder to her chest. "It can't be easy for you, doing all these happy things with that looming over you."

I dashed at my eyes; there were tears there again. The moment anyone showed kindness, it seemed, I lost it. "It's what Barry would want," I said.

She nodded again. "Doesn't make it any easier, though," she remarked.

"No," I agreed. "It doesn't." I turned away and tweaked the gauzy white curtains I'd woven into the bower. My mascara was running; I was sure of it. Nothing like carrying the funeral vibe into a wedding. *Breathe, Riley, just breathe.*

The brides and their two friends duly arrived, and I'd been right about the giggling; they were still doing it as they walked in, accompanied by music piped out of a Bluetooth speaker. Someone I'd never heard of. I made a mental note to get a little more current with my iTunes.

Jeannette was lovely, as always. "We are here today," she said, "to welcome Heather and Caroline, who have come to Provincetown to be married. Your marriage is being entered into reverently, with the recognition of the true union you have discovered together. For what greater joy is there for two human souls than to join together to strengthen each other in all their endeavors, to support each other through all sorrow, and to share with each other in all gladness?"

The two brides looked at each other and giggled. I was starting to suspect that they'd started celebrating well before the ceremony.

"I hope," said Jeannette, "that the words and spirit of this afternoon may be filled with a truth that will deepen with the passing years. I hope, too, that the meaning of the vows that you are about to share will deepen as well, as you discover the endless possibilities of this life together. Remember that you do not belong *to* each other, but rather *with* each other."

I was standing off to the side, trying to be sure I wasn't in any of the photos that Gregg was taking, when I looked straight across the patio toward the small bar that we keep there, staffed during events, and saw Barry loping by.

No. It wasn't Barry. I blinked furiously and looked again and there was no one there. A ghost? Hardly; I dismissed that at once. I've never been a big believer in some Shangri-La of an afterlife; you live, you die, end of story. More likely it was some bear staying at the inn who was hurrying through because he knew he wasn't supposed to be there. Still, it had been curious, it was exactly Barry's loping gait. Stop, I told myself. Breathe. It's not like it was Barry's signature move, or anything like that…

It's okay. Breathe. It wasn't Barry. You're just looking for a connection to him. Which was probably why people saw ghosts, in the first place.

The wedding was moving forward; Jeannette had just reached her trademark Apache benediction. "Now you will feel no rain, for each of you will be shelter to the other. Now you will feel no cold, for each of you will be warmth to the other. Now there is no more loneliness for you, but there is only one life before you. Go now to your dwelling place, to enter into the days of your togetherness, and may your days be good, and long upon the earth. Congratulations, you may now each kiss the bride!"

I scurried over to the table with the champagne and the strawberries, and poured carefully for everyone in the wedding party. The brides insisted on champagne for the officiant, and Jeannette accepted. "Lush," I whispered to her as I handed her the glass. "Prude," she whispered back.

Eventually I handed off the brides and their friends to Martin; it was his show for their luncheon. He was particularly nice to me, which immediately made me wonder why; Martin's never gratuitously nice. I ducked into the ladies' room and sure enough, there was a trail of mascara down one cheek. Marvelous. Count on him to notice everything in one sweeping glance.

I went back to the patio and cleaned up. Gregg and Jeannette were gone, and no ghostly bears were there, either. But ghosts must have been on my mind, because when somebody came up behind me and gave me a hug, I shrieked and dropped a champagne glass.

Mirela looked as shocked as I felt. "Sydney! What is wrong with you?"

"What's wrong with you?" I demanded. "Sneaking up on me like that!"

"You are not usually so nervous," she said.

"I don't usually have people trying to give me a heart attack!"

Mirela held me out at arm's length. "Okay, then," she said. "Who are you, and what have you done with Sydney Riley?"

I wasn't in the mood for humor. "I'll clean up this glass, and then you can buy me a cocktail," I said. "That's what you came over for, right?"

"Well, I was perhaps hoping that *you* might buy *me*—oh, never mind, Sydney, let's get a drink and you can tell me everything."

Five minutes later we were sitting at the bar in the restaurant. Mirela ordered a Kir Royale and I curled my lip. "I don't know how you can stand to drink that disgusting stuff." Mirela turned to the bartender, who happened to be the new guy, Gus. "She sneers at my Kir Royale. But wait until you see what she orders," she said, then held up her hand. "But, wait! I will tell you! Because Sydney always orders the same cocktail from when she was in college, for ever and always. She will order a gin and tonic."

"A gin and tonic," I told Gus, and turned to Mirela. "So what's so strange about finding something you like, and sticking with it? Besides, I've been known to drink wine, mojitos, even margaritas. I am a woman of many facets."

"Are we still talking about drinks now?"

"We're not talking about boyfriends. Not mine, anyway." I peered at her. "What is it—did you rekindle an old romance when you were home?"

"Provincetown is home," she responded automatically.

"Bulgaria is home. With your accent, you'll never convince anyone you're a native Cape Codder. So? *Did* you have an affair?" I was eager to hear. I pretty much live vicariously through Mirela's frequent and drama-filled affairs.

"Only for a little while," she said.

"Ah, okay, I see. You mean five minutes, right?" We were both on automatic, tossing small talk back and forth while we waited for our drinks. Gus delivered, we each took a sip, and then as if by common consent turned to face each other on our barstools. "So what else do you know about Barry going up to the Murchison place? And, come to that, *how* do you know anything about Barry going up to the Murchison place?"

Mirela sighed. "Please, Sydney, you think that I am new to this? Of course I am not. I do not make things up, me."

"That told me absolutely nothing at all," I complained. "Did you know that Jason's been following Barry up there?"

"This, this is not surprising," Mirela said, contemplating her cocktail. "Jason is always looking for the edge."

That was a new thought. "An edge over what? Or whom?"

"Does it matter? Jason needs to feel special. This is one way he does it. If Barry were here now, Jason would be finding a way to use what he knows."

"Mirela, Jason's my friend."

"Who was spying on your other friend," she finished. "I do not make these things up. It is not necessarily bad, you know. Perhaps forever and always, he has felt insecure. That is all it is."

"Well, I plan to find out more. Today."

Her eyes widened. "What have you got planned, Sydney? I can see there is something."

I took a sip of gin and tonic and said, somewhat complacently, "Glenn and I are going up to the Murchison estate this afternoon. We're going to find out once and for all what Barry was playing at."

She was already shaking her head. "This is a bad, a very bad idea, Sydney."

"Why? Because I'll end up knowing more than you do?"

"Because there might be something there that will break Glenn's heart. Let him be in peace. Let him believe what he wants to."

"And the truth? The truth doesn't count for anything?"

She considered it for a moment. "Is it better to be honest, or to be kind?"

It was a trick question. She knew what my answer would be. We'd already talked it out in the abstract, more than once. "To be kind," I admitted.

"But you are going anyway."

"I'm going anyway."

Mirela tried; I'll grant her that. Over the next hour she did her best to discourage me. All that it did, of course, was make me feel guilty. But it was a door I had to go through. I didn't even know why.

Which should have given me a clue, right there.

18

As I left the bar, I finally figured out that the annoying beeping sound I was hearing was actually coming from my pocket; to wit, from my smartphone. Voicemail. I pressed the relevant buttons and heard, "Hello, Sydney, this is Ali. I have something important to ask you. I'll call again later."

That rated right up there with "I have something important to tell you but I want to make you wonder about it for a while so I'm not going to say what it is." So helpful. I pressed call back, but got his voicemail, naturally. "What the hell kind of message was that?" I demanded. "If it's important, then tell me what it is! Being enigmatic doesn't become you!" So there; that really told him.

Besides, being enigmatic actually did become him.

I sped home with just enough time to brush my teeth so I wouldn't have gin breath and slip into jeans and a t-shirt. I didn't think we were going to have to make our way up the hill through the bracken, but one never knows.

The poolside was full of bears catching rays when I got back to the inn. Glenn was at the front desk, standing next to Jason, who was looking bored beyond words. "You ready?"

"I'm ready for anything, darling, you know that!"

"I think she's talking to me," Glenn told him. At least he seemed less catatonic this time; that was progress. "We can use Barry's car," he told me.

A *car*? On Commercial Street? "Um, are you sure?" I asked. "Because it's not that far to walk—"

"I'm sure," he said, cutting me off and coming out from behind the counter in case Jason had anything more to say. Clearly not in the mood for light banter.

"Okay," I said, taking the opportunity when his back was turned to do a dramatic palms-up to Jason. Sorry, dude. Jason looked like he'd give his right arm, or his first-born, to find out what we were doing. Maybe he'd find Mirela in the restaurant; they shared an incapacity to keep a secret.

Barry's car was a lovely roomy Mercedes with functioning air conditioning. Glenn seemed to know exactly where he was going; I sometimes forgot that he'd been coming to P'town for decades. "So what's the plan?" I asked.

He gave me a look. "This was your idea, right?"

"It's a good idea," I said defensively. I just hadn't gotten to the next step beyond it being a good idea.

"It might be," Glenn said, and we drove the rest of the way in slow traffic and increasingly uncomfortable silence. At the end of Commercial Street he pulled over. I looked at the gate with some trepidation. "I don't even see the buzzer," I said.

"Who needs a buzzer?"

"Um, we do, because I don't want to go over the fence and—"

Glenn pulled the keys from the ignition and dangled them in front of me. "Barry's keys."

Okay. I hadn't thought of that. I watched him go over and insert a key into the electronic box. The gate swung open. Glenn got back into the car and we started up the driveway. This was a long swooping affair that led us past two of the controversial houses before getting to the Promised Land at the top of the hill: the Gropius house.

"This will be a disappointment," Glenn remarked, "if there's no one home."

"Of course somebody's home," I said, getting out of the car. "If you lived in a house like this, wouldn't you be home?"

"I'd never live in a house like this."

"There's that," I acknowledged. It *was* a little daunting. All wood and glass and strange angles.

"Come on," said Glenn, not one to flinch in the face of battle. "Let's see what she has to say."

And as he went forward to ring the doorbell, part of me wondered, *how does he know it's a she? What does he know about Yasmina?*

The door opened, and I stopped thinking altogether.

***

She was, simply, gorgeous.

I'd been spending so much time casting Yasmina as the "bad guy" that I hadn't given much thought to her as a person. I'd never seen a picture of her and she looked perfect in the Gropius house, cool and collected and somehow organically part of a place that no one should look organically part of. I suspected that this would happen wherever she was. She was completely at home on Planet Earth.

I walked in there determined to hate her. Either she had been conniving with Barry or leading him astray, and either way it had damaged him. She'd even possibly led to his death, though I wasn't sure exactly how that would have worked.

She didn't seem surprised to see us. "You must be Glenn," she said, and shook his hand. "I am so very sorry for your loss." Glenn looked nonplussed, and I realized that he, too, had come ready to hate her.

Yasmina turned to me. "And Sydney, too, of course," she said, extending her hand. "I'm so very sorry."

I managed to find my voice. "Thank you." I took a deep breath. "And I gather we should express condolences to you, too. We never knew that you and Barry were so close."

"Ah, yes," she said, and smiled the saddest smile I think I'd ever seen. She half-turned and gestured. "Please come and sit down. I expect that you have a lot of questions."

Oh, do we ever, I thought.

We took a moment to arrange ourselves on the angular and not terribly comfortable furniture, each piece made expressly for one particular place in on particular room. Yasmina offered coffee; we both passed on it. How do you accuse someone of terrible things when you're drinking their coffee? I leaned as far forward as my chair would allow. "Mrs. Edwards—"

"Yasmina, please," she said. The name sounded more exotic when she said it. I wondered where she was from, originally. The caramel skin could have come out of anywhere.

"Okay, Yasmina," I said. "So what was going on?"

She frowned. "I don't know what—"

"Don't even try," I said. "We know that Glenn came here, frequently, over at least the past year, probably well before that. What we want to know is why." I shot a look at Glenn, but he had the dazed expression on his face again. No help there. Okay, like it or not, I had to ask the question. "What kind of relationship did the two of you have?"

"What kind—?" she started to say, and then shook her head. "Not what you're thinking. My husband and I have our differences, but they've never driven me to that extreme. And I doubt very much that I'd've been Barry's cup of tea." She looked at Glenn.

"Him being gay and monogamous and all that."

"So it was something else," I said, nodding. "Did it have to do with the green-card scam he was running out of Race Point?"

She leaned forward and picked up an ornate cigarette lighter from the table and played with it. *Why is she so nervous? You should teach her your breathing trick.* Yes," she said finally. "Yes, I knew. I was part of it."

"I knew it!" I said without thinking. "But, wait, I still don't get it. Barry didn't need to make any extra money, and we can't find any traces of where he put it when he got it. And it must have been hundreds of thousands of dollars." I glanced around. "Forgive me, but it doesn't really look like you're in need of an extra thousand or so yourself."

"It wasn't for that!" She tossed the lighter back on the table. "It didn't have anything to do with making money—at least, not for ourselves." She stood up, paced over to the floor-to-ceiling glass with the sweeping views of the marshes and Wood End Light. She looked out the window for a moment, as though steadying herself, and then turned to face us. "What do you know," she asked, "about human trafficking?"

We both gaped at her. Glenn finally found his voice. "Nothing," he said. "And neither did Barry. If you're suggesting that any of the people who came over to get married were coerced, then you can stop right there. Barry had nothing to do with that."

"I know," said Yasmina calmly. "You might not believe it yet, but we're both really on the same side." A deep breath. "Let me tell you something, give you some statistics," she said. "The fastest growing criminal enterprise in the world is trafficking women and children for sexual exploitation, despite the fact that it's against international law and the laws of one hundred and thirty-four countries." Another deep breath. She started ticking the stats off on her fingers. "At least thirty million adults and children are bought and sold worldwide into commercial sexual servitude, forced labor, and bonded labor. About two million children are exploited every year in the global commercial sex trade. Almost six in ten identified trafficking survivors were trafficked for sexual exploitation. And women and girls make up ninety-eight percent of victims of trafficking for sexual exploitation." She took a deep breath. "Here in this country, people are being bought, sold, and smuggled like modern-day slaves. They're often beaten, starved, and forced to work as prostitutes or to take jobs as migrant, domestic, restaurant, or factory workers with little or no pay."

"I feel like I'm hearing a pitch for some Save the Children kind of organization," I said, but my heart wasn't really in the sarcasm. This was bigger than I'd thought it would be, and I sure as hell hadn't seen it coming. It felt like the world was tilting off its axis, and I was trying to recover my footing.

Yasmina sensibly ignored me. "Barry and I met at some rubber-chicken dinner in Boston eleven or twelve years ago. I can't even remember what it was about. We sat next to each other through a very long and tedious dinner, and we started talking."

Eleven years ago... when Barry had started the green-card scam. Before my time at the inn.

"What we realized," said Yasmina, "was that we both wanted to do something better with our lives, something that could have a lasting positive effect on the world. We both had excellent careers, a partner who loved us, and both of our lives should have been complete."

"They should have been. But apparently it wasn't. Apparently I wasn't enough," said Glenn. "Why didn't he tell me about any of this?"

"I haven't told my husband, either," said Yasmina. "We agreed on that, too. Primarily because we didn't want you getting hurt. We cross paths with some people who—well, let's just say that it's not the safest activity in the world."

"What exactly is it?" I asked.

She pushed her shoulder off the glass and came over and sat down again. "We tried everything we could," she said. "We've each been working in different ways. We could probably have founded a nonprofit agency, but," she shrugged, "it seemed to be easier somehow to stay off the map."

"And you could operate outside the law," I murmured.

She stared at me. "Yes," she said simply. "Does that shock you? But I've learned what works and what won't work, and we felt there wasn't enough time. I've been lobbying for state and federal laws specifically prohibiting sex tourism; Hawai'i finally passed one." She looked out the window, restless. "Barry's been working directly with victims, helping them get away, get back home, finding them jobs, whatever it takes. Not everybody can return to their country of origin. Some women are doubly exploited: once when they're forced into the sex trade, and then again if they return and are ostracized as damaged goods. We've both donated personal money, but we were concerned about tax implications—well, I was, anyway. I'm a public figure, even now. So then we hit on the green-card weddings. We'd help people who immigrated here against their will though people who would pay a lot to immigrate here. It seemed—appropriate. Like everything's gone full circle."

I looked blankly at Glenn. Neither of us seemed to know what to say.

Yasmina didn't mind. "Let me tell you more," she said. I had the impression that it wasn't the first time she'd given this speech. "Trafficking in persons has three constituent elements. There's the act: recruitment, transportation, transfer, harboring or receipt of persons. Then there's the means: the threat or use of force, coercion, abduction, fraud, deception, abuse of power or vulnerability, or giving payments or benefits to a person in control of the victim. And finally there's the purpose: exploitation, which includes sexual exploitation, forced labor, slavery, that sort of thing." She smiled at nothing. "Even the removal of organs. They don't care who has to die, as long as it's not them."

A memory flashed through my brain: breakfast with Julie at Chach's, and her voice, flat and expressionless: *"But most of the time, people who don't follow the rules, it's because they think they're better than the rest of us, or different from the rest of us. They're above all that. So whatever they want, they feel justified in getting. They steal stuff. They text when driving. They kill somebody. Because everyone else is just a backdrop to their lives. We're the bit players; they're the stars. Why should they lose sleep? They got what they wanted.*" I could only think that those were exactly the people who trafficked in human lives.

Yasmina seemed restless; she got up and went to the window again. "Virtually every country in the world is affected by this crime. Origin countries, transit countries, or destination countries. Criminals operated everywhere." She sounded like she had had to convince people in the past. "Smuggled migrants are vulnerable to everything. They take life-threatening risks and are constantly exploited because they have no legal standing. Thousands of people have suffocated in containers, perished in deserts, or dehydrated at sea. Migrant smuggling fuels corruption and empowers organized crime. And it generates huge profits for the criminals involved."

I roused myself. "So what are you saying? That one of them came after Barry?"

She looked at me, expressionless. "You tell me."

19

"They couldn't have," I said. "Seriously, *Glenn* didn't know Barry was doing anything like this. *I* didn't know Barry was doing anything like this. How would somebody who doesn't know him as well as we do figure out what he was doing? It just doesn't make sense."

"He's known," said Yasmina. "In the places where it matters, he's known. Some really bad people know about him. Arrests have been made. Some people have lost fortunes because of him. He's on the trafficker's Most Wanted List. As am I." I must have been looking askance at her, because she came back over, sat down, and leaned forward in her chair, the better—apparently—to convince me. "Listen, we both know that Provincetown is, at the bottom of it all, really just a small town. And the whole issue of human trafficking is so much wider. What kind of criminals do we have here? Bicycle thieves. Possibly some folks cheating on their income tax. A couple of people riding the system. The occasional DUI." She shook her head. "This is so much bigger, Sydney. Millions of dollars are involved, and money is the only thing that matters in the current cultural context."

I didn't need her to spell out the current cultural context.

"And don't think that doesn't affect the discourse, that closing our borders is going to affect illegal immigration—the *real* illegal immigration—in any way at all. Do people really think that all the migrant workers in California are there voluntarily? Does anyone seriously imagine that a twelve-year-old in a brothel had any choice in the matter? The conversation hasn't yet touched on the real crime behind immigration, and I doubt that it will. But Barry knew. Barry was willing to risk his life to change the world." Her voice caught on a sob and she turned her face away.

"You really did love each other," I said. "Just not in the way I'd thought."

Glenn looked at me and then got up and crossed the room, sitting down next to Yasmina, putting an arm around her shoulders. She turned and cried softly into his shoulder. Over her head, our eyes met. "Yasmina," said Glenn, "Thank you."

I blinked tears out of my own eyes. I couldn't just sit there watching them hold each other, it was treading on too much intimacy that had nothing to do with me. I took a cue from Yasmina and got up and went to the window. The sun was bright and blinding. There were a lot of people on the breakwater, far enough away to be indistinguishable from my height. Funny to think of all those people living their lives oblivious to the secrets that moved below the surface, like a creature from the deep, on the same plane but in a different universe.

The concept had yet to sink in. I'd loved Barry, for sure, but Barry as *hero*? He was an affable bear. He made jokes and cared about his friends and family and loved his inn and his town fiercely; but saving lives? Risking God-only-knew-what if his green card scam was uncovered?

But of course it had been uncovered. Ali Hakim had uncovered it. Who else knew? How close had Barry been to being arrested? I didn't have to ask how close he had been to getting killed… "That has to be it," I said to the view. "God, it opens up a whole new can of worms, doesn't it? Suspects everywhere you look."

"The police will never find them," said Yasmina. "They're buried under shell corporations, names under names under names. Even if the investigation goes to the state police, they don't have the kind of budget you'd need to go after these people. You have no idea how rich they are."

That was good, coming from someone who lived in a Gropius house, but I let it slide. "So what do we do?" I asked, turning away from the window.

"I do not know," said Yasmina. "But I will not stop. Not now. I cannot."

"Because of Barry?"

"Because," she said in a voice that was suddenly very small, "it is how I came to America."

I stared at her. Well, it made sense, but damn… "I'm sorry," I said, inadequately, and I saw Glenn tighten his arm around her.

"It is the past," she said simply. "But the scars—physical, yes, and emotional—they last forever. It is a part of who I am."

It was none of my business, but I asked anyway. "Where are you from? Where did this happen?"

"From Beirut," she said. "This happened in Lebanon."

Lebanon? Where a certain ICE agent's parents were from? I believed in coincidence, but this…I looked at Glenn. "We should go," I said.

And all the way back to the inn, all I could think of was Ali.

***

Glenn dropped me off at the entrance. "I have some things to do," he said vaguely, and I hopped out. As soon as he drove off, I punched up Mirela's contact on my smartphone. "You were wrong!" I said.

"Hello, again, to you, too," she said.

"Hello," I said impatiently. "Is that better?"

"Yes, it is. And I am rarely wrong."

"You are this time. Barry wasn't in love with Yasmina, so there! He didn't cheat on Glenn." Well, other than the odd hook-up, but that was part of their deal. "It's exactly as I thought."

"Well, well," she said thoughtfully. "You do surprise me."

"You always have your mind in the gutter," I complained. "Sometimes a banana is just a banana!"

"Please? Is that an idiom?"

One I didn't really want to explore. "I don't think I can tell you about it, but take it from me, Barry was actually doing something very good," I said instead. "He and Yasmina had a—a project—together. They were both dedicated to it."

"So it *was* about sex trafficking!"

"I didn't say that! Where did you get that ideas?"

"Oh, please, Sydney, you forget where I am from. In Eastern Europe, many women disappear to the USA. Some as housemaids. Some as prostitutes. They don't know that, naturally, they come here for what they believe is an honest job. And then they find out that they are slaves."

"Do you know anyone that happened to?" I asked.

"Everyone in Bulgaria knows someone that happened to," she said soberly.

Wow. Have you ever noticed how when you encounter some new experience, suddenly you run into traces of it everywhere? I'm stunned by how often it happens. "I'm sorry for that," I said, inadequately, as if by being American I was tainted by other Americans who still thought that human beings could be bought or sold.

"You do not have to be sorry," she said. "You are not part of it."

"I'm part of the people who ignore it," I said. All right, yeah, so I was raised Catholic. I may not go to Mass every week, but I still do guilt exceedingly well. Besides, I *did* feel shame. The more Yasmina was talking, the more I wondered why this was such an invisible crime. Why weren't people out on the streets because of it? The same people who would decry slavery in the antebellum south were apparently on board with the same thing if it involved an Asian child or an Eastern European woman.

Mirela said, "Sydney? You are still there?"

I swallowed. "I'm still here," I said. "Seriously, Mirela, how did you guess that's what it was? It might be important."

"I have had conversations with Barry," she said, "where I—what is the expression, to read on top of the print?"

What? "Read between the lines?"

"Yes. I read between the lines. Because I know Barry, and as I said, I am familiar with the practice. So many of these people are either coming to America or part of sex tourism that includes Americans, yet the USA does not talk much about it. Everyone wants to think that here it is Disneyland every day."

She wasn't wrong. I sighed. "Why on earth did you want to become a citizen, of this country, anyway?"

"You think that it's better anywhere else? All right: Germany, perhaps. I like Germany. But I can do my art here. Oh, yes, art! I remember art! That thing that I was doing when you called."

"You didn't have to answer."

"You would have called again and again until I did."

Yet again, she wasn't wrong. "All right. Get back to it. What are you working on?"

"It will become many sailboats. But not yet. For today, just the background will make me happy."

"Okay," I said. "See you tomorrow."

"Tomorrow?"

I felt my stomach muscles tighten. "Barry's funeral." *Breathe, Riley, just breathe through it.*

"Ah, yes. This I will not miss. I will see you tomorrow, Sydney."

And then my phone rang again.

20

It was Ali.

"About time!" I exclaimed. "I need to talk to you." And, I added silently, ask *you* a few questions, too.

"Good timing, then. I'll be in Provincetown in an hour. Would you like to have dinner?"

"You mean, as a witness, or as a date?"

"You never make things easy," he complained. "Does it matter what we call it?"

"Of course it does," I said. "I'm basing my wardrobe on your answer."

A chuckle. "All right. Have it your way. Let's call it a date with some serious conversation thrown in."

"What was the question you wanted to ask me? When you called me before and left that enigmatic message?"

"At dinner," he said. "You choose the place and make a reservation. I'll pick you up at six."

"Oh, hell," I said, remembering. "I have a *wedding* at six!"

"I'll still come," he said. "We can have an *après*-wedding dinner."

I found myself smiling. "Okay."

The wedding was ten people, all of them bears, which was probably delighting the restaurant staff; bears eat more and tip well. There was a harpist, already out on the patio at 5:30 when I got there to set out the chairs. The florists had come and gone and the bower was beautifully decorated. Sometimes I feel that everyone else does most of the work at a wedding, then I remember the hours I've spent on the phone, locking down details, negotiating with vendors, everything. Okay, yeah, now that I mention it, I *do* earn my money.

I didn't know the harpist except for setting her up with the gig, so we chatted for a while and then I put out the champagne, glasses, and strawberries, and assembled the materials for the glass ceremony they'd chosen to be part of the wedding. (What happens is that the couple pours from two separate containers holding different colors of glass beads into one vase, symbolic of their blending together, then later that gets sent off to be placed in an oven so that the glass all fuses together into a unique glass sculpture. It's actually quite lovely.)

Gus the bartender arrived and opened up the wedding-patio bar, and almost immediately guys from the wedding party drifted in and started ordering drinks, affable, laughing together. Gus offered me one, smiling his very white smile, and I wondered yet again what his story was. Didn't wonder enough to ask him, of course. I just shook my head and kept circulating, greeting the bears and moving them as unobtrusively as I could toward their seats facing the bower.

Vernon breezed in close to the last minute as I was beginning to have grim thoughts about the whole thing—and him in particular. "There you are, Missy-poo," he said, giving me a hug. "Lady Di to the rescue."

"You wouldn't have to rescue me if you got here early," I pointed out through gritted teeth. At least the bears had brought their own photographer so I didn't have to keep up with one single more person. I was suddenly feeling exhausted.

And just as the couple, looking resplendent in matching tuxes, was coming down the aisle to the haunting silvery sound of the harp, Ali walked in. He was looking amused and I tried not to smile in response. He stayed over by the bar, out of the way, but seemed prepared to settle in. He was wearing a suit again, something in dark gray, and he looked, frankly, terrific.

You really don't like him, remember?

Vernon was managing not to call the couple anything untoward, though he did once or twice slip in his trademarked phrase, "Sweet Sarah and Oh Petunias." (Don't ask me what it means. I haven't the faintest idea.) Vows were made, rings were exchanged, glass grains were poured, everyone applauded. I served champagne and, when the wedding party was busy with toasts, poured an extra glass and held it up toward Ali. He shook his head, still smiling. He was an enigma. Most people would trip over their own feet to sample some Perrier-Jouët. I'd bought it myself, and knew that each of these bottles cost well over two hundred dollars. But maybe that's just me. Maybe ICE agents made more than I thought and he drank Perrier-Jouët every night.

I was just tidying up after they'd all trooped out to the restaurant, officiant and harpist in tow, when my phone rang. "Sydney Riley," I said.

"Sydney, this is Julie. How're you doing?"

"Much better, thanks." And amazingly, I was. I felt like a weight had been lifted off me since we'd spoken to Yasmina.

"Good, good," she said. "I'll be there for the funeral tomorrow."

"Oh, good. Thanks, Julie. Barry would be pleased if he knew." He would, too. Barry and Julie liked each other.

"I wanted to tell you," she said. "The state police have gotten involved, they're in on the investigation. Probably taking the lead, in fact. We're not ending anything just because he's buried."

"I didn't think you would." I remembered that Ali was there, and gave him a hands-up helpless gesture. He just smiled.

"What I wanted to ask was if you knew where Gus Danforth is," she said. "He's not scheduled to be on at the inn, but he's also not at home."

Gus, the perennially enigmatic bartender. "Gus? Really? He was here twenty minutes ago. I mean, here, where I am, out on the wedding terrace. He served drinks before the ceremony started, then he closed up. I don't know if he's still here. He might have gone home." I paused. "Why, Julie? Are you thinking that Gus—"

"We just want another conversation with him," she said smoothly. Everything Julie does is smooth.

"Was he bartending the party? When—" I swallowed "—when Barry was killed?"

"He was there, yes," she said. "I'm sending someone over to the inn, Sydney. They'll be as discreet as possible."

I could imagine Mike's horror. "Thanks, Julie. I appreciate that." I thought about it for a moment. "You're sure there's nothing you can tell me?"

"Not yet. Sorry. Gotta go. See you tomorrow."

"See you tomorrow," I echoed, feeling completely unsatisfied. I walked over to the now-closed bar where Ali was still sitting. "So this is what you do," he said.

"This is what I do. Exciting, isn't it?"

"I imagine," he said, "that sometimes it is." He slid off the stool, leaned in and kissed my cheek. "Where are we going to dinner?"

"Café Edwige," I said. "Just down the street."

He raised his eyebrows. "Amazing," he said. "You must have some pull. Even I know that you can't get a same-day reservation there."

"And how would you know that? Three days ago you'd probably never have heard of Provincetown."

"I catch on quick," he said. "Shall we go?"

Café Edwige is above a funky clothing shop on Commercial Street, and Ali was right: I couldn't have gotten a same-day reservation there for love or money. That was why I had Mirela. She knew the owner, she knew the chef, she probably knew the dishwasher; Mirela knows everyone. I explained this to Ali as we were shown to our table, a booth right up again the open window looking down on Commercial Street. Prime real estate. Thanks, Mirela.

The waiter came and I ordered a glass of wine and Ali ordered tonic water with a twist. I wondered if he might be spending some of his time with friends of Bill; AA is a major activity here in town, so it's understandable that was my immediate reaction. Most of our liquor stores are open year-round, despite the drop in population in the off-season, and they're never hurting for business. Barry used to say that there's a type of person who's attracted to land's end, to that place where you end up when you can't run any farther, and he may have been right. Provincetown is a destination; you don't stop here on your way anywhere else, and no one got here by accident. That means it attracts both those who have excellent mental health and those who…don't.

We both stared at our menus until the waiter came back. I ordered the Coquille St. Jacques (local scallop, farmer's mushrooms, gruyere cheese, cognac, just a plateful of heaven) and Ali went for the Carbonara Edwige. "All right," I said as soon as he left. "What's the important thing you wanted to ask me?"

"Oh, good. I see that we decided against the small talk, after all," said Ali.

"You did say that it was a date with some serious conversations," I reminded him. "For example, I want to talk about immigration, forced and otherwise, and I'd like you to tell me what the important thing is you wanted to ask me. Then we can see about the rest."

He sipped his vile concoction. "All right," he said at last. "A deal's a deal. What do you know about immigration?"

"That's it? That's what you want to know? You called me and left me a curious message and the important question was how much I keep up with the news?"

"It's a pre-question question," he assured me. "Working up to it. I believe in taking my time."

Man, I certainly wasn't going to go *there*. "I know what most people know," I said cautiously. "I know that very few Latin Americans are currently coming into this country illegally and President Tweet responded by starting to build an expensive wall to keep out the people who don't want to come in. I know that the worst humanitarian crisis of all time is happening in Syria and that the US apparently thinks that a whole lot of displaced wounded children constitute a major threat to our homeland." I paused. "I know that Barry was running a green-card business on the side, and that he was funneling all of that money into a private effort to stop human trafficking."

Ali nodded. "That's a good start."

I'd been rather pleased with myself for the thoroughness of my answer. "Try and restrain your enthusiasm," I urged him.

That smile, again. Hot damn, this man was sexy. I had to remind myself that he was still, in theory anyway, the Enemy. "The real problem isn't the wall," said Ali.

"Really? My tax dollars at work?" I countered. "I'd say it's a problem."

He shrugged. "It's a problem, sure, but it's not the major one. The major one is the attempts to ban Muslims from coming into the country."

"Wait a moment," I said. "Who *are* you? I could have sworn I was talking to an ICE agent. Aren't you the guys carrying out that ban?"

He wasn't ruffled. "We do a lot of good, too," he said mildly.

"Which brings us to the main event of the evening," I said. "A friendly conversation with Customs and Immigration."

The waiter brought our dinners then, hovering to see if we needed anything else. As soon as he left, I took a first tentative bite. Yes: heaven.

"All right," said Ali. "Your hostility notwithstanding, I do think you can help me here."

I swallowed the bite and said, "I *live* to help the government."

He patted his lips with his napkin and ignored my remark. "So when I first came out here a few days ago, my assignment was to arrest Barry Parker for facilitation. We already had a case against him on paper, and we'd interviewed several witnesses who the US Attorney planned to subpoena at trial. It was a pretty dull case on the face of it."

I couldn't resist. "Until you met me," I said.

A quicksilver smile. "Until I met you," he agreed. "And, of course, Barry's murder ramped it way up as well."

"I've been meaning to thank you for getting your sister involved, for moving everything along quickly," I said. "I don't know that Glenn could have held out much longer."

"It was the least I could do, seeing as I am apparently *persona non grata* here."

"Don't take it personally," I said encouragingly. "We don't discriminate. We pretty much dislike any government agency *a priori.*" So there: he wasn't the only one who could slip a little Latin into the conversation.

"So I started investigating from another angle," Ali said. "It may be trite but it's also true: following the money is the best strategy. And I found out where the money from the scam was going."

"You met Yasmina," I said.

"I met Yasmina," he agreed. "And we had some very productive conversations. Human trafficking isn't my department, but ICE is very committed to the fight against traffickers and to victim resettlement. Ms. Edwards opened a door on two different rings that we didn't even know existed. Moving forward, she's going to be very helpful to us."

"And she's Lebanese. Like your parents," I said.

He smiled. "She's Lebanese, just like my parents," he agreed. "But that's where the similarities end. My parents *chose* to make a life in America. They went through a long process to become citizens. Ms. Edwards had little choice in the matter."

"So the Lebanese connection, that's just a coincidence?" *Holy hell, Riley,* I said to myself. *You're not actually jealous here, are you? Breathe, just breathe.*

He sipped his drink. I was in the meantime letting one of the best meals in the world go cold, and I committed the extreme heresy of shoveling in a couple of mouthfuls without tasting them. "So that's all good," I said finally. "But it doesn't get us any closer to Barry's murder."

"Possibly not. But let's not make any assumptions yet." He drew in a deep breath, released it. "Mr. Parker was connecting with a ring that runs out of Boston," he said. "They specialize in unpaid household help for the affluent residents of places like Beacon Hill and Back Bay. And the South End," he added, as though that had special significance.

And maybe it did. The South End of Boston—not to be confused with South Boston—is a gay-dominated enclave in the city.

Once home to crumbling tenements and featuring drug deals as its local industry, it had been completely transformed in the 1990s as wealthy gay men in particular started buying up property and converting it into stylish condos. It wasn't long before the restaurants and art galleries and florists followed, and now the area is upscale and stylish. During its transformation nobody really noticed where all the residents who were forced out ended up going; that's never part of the equation.

But what really caught my attention was that a lot of second homes in P'town are owned by residents of the South End. "So," I said softly. "Someone was on to Barry."

"It's possible," said Ali. "We've actually traced someone specific. He's here in Provincetown now, for the season. We've been watching him for a while in connection with another case, and then made the connection with this one. He's deeply involved. He bought both his condos—and another one on Fire Island—on the backs of women who sleep in closets, are given near-starvation portions of food, and who spend their days cleaning, scrubbing, whatever…" He stopped himself for a moment; his voice had cracked on that last bit. "Anyway," he said at length, "Mr. Parker was not exactly his best friend. Between them, Mr. Parker and Ms. Edwards were threatening a very lucrative business and a luxurious lifestyle, and this guy somehow found out about them." Another pause. "They bring them over in storage containers, you know."

"So I've gathered." My Public Enemy Number One was turning into a man of principles and courage in front of my eyes; the frog into the prince. "But if he killed Barry, isn't Yasmina at risk now? Please tell me that someone's keeping an eye on her!"

"We're doing the best we can," he said. "I can't be more specific."

I couldn't imagine how anyone could keep an eye on her up at that estate, with its long winding driveway and hills of trees and bracken. But that was his wheelhouse, not mine. I finished my coquille St.-Jacques in silence. The fear that was flashing through me for Yasmina was battling dinner for dominance in my gut.

"So all of this to get around to what I wanted to ask you," said Ali, reaching into an inner pocket. He pulled out a photograph and slid it across the table to me. "Here's the guy. His name's Anthony Avery. Have you seen him around the inn?"

I inspected it. Tall guy, mid-forties at a guess, blond hair and blue eyes. Reasonably attractive. I wanted to impale him on my dinner knife. "No," I said. I can't remember seeing him. Though a lot of people come and go, I really only see the ones involved with weddings."

"He wouldn't have been staying there," said Ali. "Just figuring out how to get close to Mr. Parker. Are you sure?"

What, I'm going to suddenly change my mind? I nodded and slid the photograph back across the table. "I'm sure," I said.

"I should tell you that your colleague Mr. Griffiths has positively identified him. He says that he sees everyone who comes and goes, and that this individual was there more than once over the past month."

"If Jason says so, then it's probably true," I said. "He works ridiculous hours and he pays attention to everybody. Especially someone with looks like those." I nodded toward the photograph. But I was still sure I hadn't seen him.

"All right," said Ali, putting the photo back in his pocket and signaling the waiter. "Would you like coffee? Dessert?"

I shook my head. I didn't need anything keeping me awake. Ali asked for the check and said, "I've requested a transfer, by the way."

I was surprised by the jolt of disappointment that went through me. "You did? To where?"

"To the human trafficking division of Homeland Security," he said. "I'll stay in the Boston office, but with a different department. I've learned more in the past few days than I ever wanted to know. And I want to do something about it."

I tried not to show my relief. "I'm seriously impressed," I told him; and then, as he kept watching me, "What?"

"Just waiting for the other shoe to drop," he said. "This is definitely your cue for more sarcasm."

"No sarcasm. I really am impressed." I smiled. "You're coming over to the good guys, Ali."

We went down the stairs and back into the eddying currents of humanity on Commercial Street. People were out hawking their shows, drag queens and young men clad only in towels around their waist and the latest in the Broadway series at the Crown. Street musicians vied with each other for the crowd's attention. My phone rang. "Sorry," I said to Ali. "I can't not answer."

He waved me on. It was a text message: STAY AWAY FROM THE MURCHISON ESTATE IF YOU VALUE YOUR LIFE. Ali caught the expression on my face and I turned the phone so he could read it. "Text back," he said. "Ask who they are."

I obediently punched in the letters and sent the message. We sat down on one of the benches in front of town hall and waited. Ali pulled out his phone and keyed in a number. "Hi, Claire, it's Ali," he said. "I need a trace on a number." He reached out for my phone and I handed it to me. "508-555-9830," he said. "Yeah, right now. There's been a threat. Okay. Thanks."

He disconnected and looked at my phone again. "Don't think they're the chatty type," he said.

"What is going on?" Despite the heat of the evening, I was suddenly feeling very cold.

"If you value your life," he quoted. "Sounds like someone who reads too many thrillers. Bad thrillers." He keyed another contact on his phone. "Ali here. Anything? No? Okay, I've got a threat here. Not against the subject, someone else, but it's warning her away from the Murchison place." A pause as he listened. "Okay. Grab someone else to get up there with you, and keep an eye out."

"Shouldn't we do something?" I asked.

"We are doing something," he said. "I've increased the guard on Ms. Edwards. And—" He broke off as his telephone rang. "Agent Hakim," he said. "Right. I could have predicted it. Thanks anyway."

"What was that?"

"Burner phone," he said. "Can't be traced. Anyway, she's safe for tonight. And I'll go up again tomorrow."

"I'm coming with you," I said.

"Um—we *were* reading the same text on your phone, weren't we?"

"What text?" I asked, all innocence. "Oh, come on, Ali. I have to. If this guy killed Barry, then he's not going to stop until he gets Yasmina, too."

"I did manage to gather the same impression," said Ali. "But that's a great reason for *me* to look into it, not you."

"The text came to me. You'll want to know if he calls or texts me again, won't you?"

"Are you serious? You're *blackmailing* me?" But he looked amused, not angry. "All right, Wonder Woman, you can come."

"Jason called me Wonder Woman too," I said.

Ali nodded. "So it must be true," he said.

21

The sky wept for Barry the day of his funeral.

Actually, the sky went berserk: one of our few real summer storms, with dark clouds and hammering rain and occasional lightning flashing across the sky and thunder shaking the ground. Quite a display.

The funeral was at Gately's since neither Barry nor Glenn practiced any religious tradition; and we'd closed down the dining room at the inn for the post-funeral gathering. There was no wake and no open casket, "best," said Glenn, "to remember him as he was." The expression may have been trite, but it was the only decision there could be; I was still seeing Barry's face imprinted in my brain every time I closed my eyes at night.

The place was standing-room-only, and not a lot of that. I was so grateful: over the years, Barry had helped a lot of people, in small and large and amazing ways, and they were all here. Bears, of course; lots of them. I spotted Tim and Franco, who'd gotten married at the inn my first year there. And of course Lukas and Henry. And Glenn seemed to be surrounded by ursine friends.

But the woman from the parking lot where he left his car was there, and the guys from Far Land where he got his lunch sandwich every day, and his favorite teller from Seamen's Bank, and absolutely *everyone* who worked at Race Point. "He'd be pleased, don't you think?" asked Mike. "He'd probably snarl at everyone to get back to work," I said. Barry had been a true bear, a little rough and growling on the outside, warm and cuddly on the inside.

There had been so much going on the past week, adrenaline-fueled days of trying to see if I could help figure out who'd killed him, that I'd put my feelings on a shelf somewhere. The problem with doing that, of course, is that when you take them down they're as fresh and sharp as ever. I couldn't imagine what life was going to be like without Barry. Things at the inn would shake out; his work with Yasmina would continue; we'd all carry on. But it felt suddenly like a lonely world, this one that didn't have Barry in it.

Julie caught up with me at the reception, balancing a cup of coffee with one of Adrienne's fancy pastries. "So you found Gus?" I asked conversationally.

She shook her head. "He's gone."

"What do you mean, gone?"

"I mean gone. Packed up his apartment and took off. Last seen getting gas at Cumberland Farms," she said. "That kind of gone."

"So what do you do now? Are you thinking it might've been him?"

"I don't know," Julie said. "I think there's a good chance that he might have been stealing money from the inn—there seemed to be a lot of irregularities in the bar take, as well as the other stuff missing. Mike and I sat down and went through them and I'd bet that if he's done that, he's done more. We'll find him," she added confidently.

"But you don't think he killed Barry?"

"I'm inclined to share Agent Hakim's opinion. We're thinking it probably had to do with the trafficking. There's a lot of money riding on this, somewhere. But we'll see what Gus says when we track him down." She sighed and looked around. "And you'll see that at the end, it will be all about your famous lucre after all. Someone who thought his life was more important than scores of other ones, and didn't want anyone getting in their way."

"It's a terrible way to die," I said. I wasn't talking about the antifreeze.

"But don't you see?" she asked. "In the end, he won. Barry stopped this guy, one way or the other. He won't be smuggling any more people in from a jail cell. So Barry got what he wanted in the end."

It made sense. Sort of. Might be the best outcome we could pull from the whole mess. "We're going up to see Yasmina today," I told her.

She nodded. "I know. I'll be going up there too. We all need to have a conversation about keeping her safe, and getting the kind of evidence we need against Anthony Avery."

The name was familiar. "Avery?"

"Anthony Avery. The man Agent Hakim has identified as being out to get Barry and Yasmina."

There was something about the way she said Yasmina's name that probably should have tipped me off, but didn't. "So," I said with only a trace—I promise—of malice, "ICE and the local police force *can* cooperate, after all." Provincetown's police force (well,

Julie, anyway) had made it clear they weren't going to be an extension of ICE.

"Provincetown police, the district attorney's office, the Massachusetts state police, and ICE," she said, nodding. "Nothing short of a miracle. But I have to say I was surprised. Agent Hakim is actually human, or at least plays one on TV."

For reasons that I still don't understand, I blushed. "He's transferring to the trafficking department at Homeland Security," I said.

Julie looked at me appraisingly. "So that's how it is," she said.

"That's how *what* is?" *Don't overact, Riley.*

She just gave me her best Mona Lisa smile. "I'll see you later, Sydney. Agent Hakim just arrived."

"Julie—" But she had already turned away with her coffee and her pastry, so I looked toward the door. Ali was indeed there, and drenched to the bone. I wondered what he'd been doing, and where he's been doing it, between the funeral and arriving here. I'd seen him at Gately's. Another suit. He really wasn't getting the memo about how we dress. "You look like you need a towel," I said.

"It's raining out, or didn't you notice?" He ran a hand through his hair. "So much for fun in the sun."

"We can't actually control the weather," I said. "Listen, you know that Julie's going up to Yasmina's place this afternoon too, right?"

He nodded. "Yasmina was at the funeral. My guy nearly blew a fuse trying to stay with her and still scan the crowd. We told her she'd be better off for now staying away from this." This being, of course, the even greater crowd that had surged into the inn to eat and drink and tell Barry stories to each other.

"Julie seems to know her well."

He shot me a look. "You do know, don't you?"

"Know what?"

"You live in Provincetown and you work on same-sex weddings and you have the worst gaydar on the planet," he said.

"I know I do," I said automatically, then put a hand on his arm. "Wait, Ali—Yasmina's married!"

"A marriage of convenience. She got her her citizenship through her husband. He gets to have her play hostess at the parties he throws."

"Is he gay?" He'd have to be, to consider marriage to the lovely Yasmina a marriage of convenience.

Ali shook his head. "It's complicated," he said. "Let's just say that he doesn't expect any intimacy with Yasmina. Which is convenient, since she prefers her lovers female." There was water trickling down his face from his wet hair. "You *did* know about Julie, right?"

"Well, yeah, of course." I had to manage some sort of dignity—not to mention credibility—here.

"There you go." He turned and scanned the room. Way too many people, I thought, to be able to see anyone specific.

"So is Julie going because she's a detective or because she's into Yasmina?" I asked.

"It's always nice," murmured Ali, "to mix business and pleasure. Speaking of which, I'm going to get something to eat before it all disappears."

I watched him go, looking slight among all the bears. A sudden clap of thunder and the lights went out for a second before the generator kicked in. In the moment between the two, jagged lightning illuminated the room and a hand landed on my shoulder. I came close to screaming. "It's getting really miserable out there," said Jason.

"You can't creep up on people like that," I complained. "Giving me a heart attack."

He smiled. "Thought you'd recognize the scent," he said. "My Miller Harris. It's not like you haven't mentioned it before."

Jason and I regularly had several conversations about all sorts of thing that he owned, wore, said, or did. But I did remember asking him how on earth he could afford his favorite Tangerine Vert, which even on eBay (I'd looked it up one wintry day when I had nothing better to do) was selling for four hundred dollars. "A man needs a signature cologne," he'd said, and then laughed. "Relax, Sydney, I didn't rob a bank. I have some very…generous friends."

Didn't want to go *there*. No, thank you very much. As I said, Jason's sex life would terrify me if I ever came close to understanding it. And now that he'd mentioned it, I could recognize the scent. "Anyway," I said, "it's a nice turnout for Barry."

"Yes, indeedy. Did you see that Dan Wolf is here?" Celebrity spotting is another of Jason's hobbies.

"I saw," I acknowledged. Dan Wolf is the owner of Cape Air and a former Massachusetts senator.

"*And* the mayor of Boston," Jason went on. "*And* that lovely boy from the underwear commercials," he added.

"For heaven's sake," I said impatiently. "This is Barry's party, remember?"

"And I plan to enjoy myself at it, sweetie," he said.

I shook my head. "You're incorrigible," I told him. "I have to go, anyway."

"Where're you off to?" he asked, not looking at me, still scanning the crowd for someone impressive for his mental scrapbook.

"Ali and I are going up to the Murchison place," I said. "He's convinced me that Barry's killer is connected to what they were doing up there."

Jason turned to me then. "And what *were* they doing up there?" he asked.

I shook my head. "Too complicated to explain right now."

"Ah, I know," he said. "You want a grand dénouement, à la Hercule Poirot. You'll get everyone together and you'll say, *You may wonder why I've called you all here tonight.* Isn't that how it goes?"

I don't read mysteries. Maybe I should start. "Something like that, I suppose," I said.

"Well, the best of luck to you, honey." He gave me a quick hug. "I'm off to do some hunting of my own." He was back to scanning the crowd again. "You're incorrigible," I informed him again, and slipped away.

22

The rain hadn't let up one little bit by the time we left Race Point Inn, and there was a tremendous clap of thunder just as we headed out the door. I jumped, and Ali put his arm around me. It felt protective. It felt good. I reacted by pulling away from him. He might be beautiful, he might be smart, he might be showing his human side, but I'd been married once to someone else with a human side and had no intention of starting down *that* road again.

The wedding lady doesn't exactly practice what she preaches.

Ali drove his sister's big muscle car, and the rain was hammering on the roof. Hard. "This is ridiculous," I said, cringing as another flash of lightning was followed almost immediately by a crash of thunder; the storm was right on top of us. "I feel like we're driving up to the Addams house."

"I always liked that Morticia," Ali said mildly.

"I'll just bet you did." I gave him a quelling look.

"I was jealous as hell of Gomez."

"You had," I pronounced, "a very strange childhood."

"True enough."

I peered at him. "I'm really glad that you're transferring," I said.

"Yeah? So you could hold your head up when you're seen with the wicked ICE agent?" There was a trace of bitterness in his voice.

Well, perhaps I'd earned it, that bitterness. "I'm sorry. This whole hostility probably wouldn't have happened in the past. But now that we get instant news from everywhere, and people post their most virulent thoughts on Facebook..." My voice trailed off and I rallied a little. "But it's also caring," I said. "Isn't it? I mean, I don't even know anyone who's Muslim, but I see how horrible a Muslim travel ban would be."

"You're wrong,"

"What do you mean, I'm wrong?" Damn, and just as I was getting used to him in his new role of caped crusader. "You think there *ought* to be a ban?"

"You're wrong that you don't know anyone who's Muslim," he said.

I stared at him while the obvious slammed me in the face. "That's why you don't drink alcohol," I said stupidly. I've rarely felt more dense. *Breathe, Riley. Just breathe.*

He nodded. "We don't all look alike," he said with a smile that didn't really look like a smile.

I swallowed. "I'm sorry. I just couldn't imagine a Muslim working for ICE."

I was only digging myself in deeper. "You ought to check that chip on your shoulder sometime," Ali said mildly, and then his voice changed. "And here we are."

The gate was unlocked and open, and we drove slowly up the winding driveway. There were a couple of cars parked in beside the garage door of the lower level of the Gropius house, which was lit up brightly in the dark afternoon. "Your guys?" I asked. Ali didn't look happy about them.

"No; they're over at one of the other houses. The only one not occupied right now," said Ali, but he still looked like he was doing sums in his head.

A shiver ran down my back. "It's him, then? I asked. "What's his name—Avery Something?"

"Anthony Avery. And I don't know." But then to my alarm he pulled a gun from under his jacket, did something to it that looked and sounded dangerous, and opened his car door, the rain lashing in. "I'd like you to stay here until I see what's what," he told me.

"Not a chance," I said. My refusal had absolutely nothing to do with bravery; I was imagining the handsome guy from Ali's photo getting out of one of those cars and creeping up on me. The last thing I wanted in that moment was to be alone.

"All right." Smart man; he knew when to argue and when to just go with the flow. "Stay behind me. You hear me? No matter what happens in there, I want you to stay behind me."

"No argument from me." I opened my door and the wind grabbed it and nearly whipped it out of my hands. Two seconds out and I was soaked. Lightning flashed. I was, apparently, trapped in a very bad horror movie.

I followed Ali up the flagstone pathway. There wasn't much we could do to stay invisible, not with that expanse of glass, but the lights were bright and so perhaps it wasn't that easy to see the two of us in the dark afternoon light. The wind was whipping my wet hair into my face, and I was completely aware of my heart pumping way too fast. *How ignoble would it be to have a heart attack here? Breathe, Riley. Just breathe.*

Ali stood to one side of the door and motioned me behind him. His gun was still out. I crouched down to the side, and he tried the handle. It turned. In all the crime dramas on TV, the handle opened, too. I always thought that was a silly fiction to make the detectives look good. Though, come to think of it, anyone attempting to break into my apartment would find that the door handle turned, too, since I never lock the place. *Wow, Riley, how many more irrelevant thoughts can you crowd into your head?*

Anything to not be present in this moment.

Ali eased himself through the door and I eased on in after him, pleased to at least be away from the sheets of rain blowing into me. This had to be a nor'easter, though they were uncommon in the summer. The timing couldn't have been worse. We crept silently across the entrance area and into the large living area, the house's interior lights making the wood come warmly alive. It was brighter than anything else in there.

I really noticed the polished wood around Yasmina, because she was sitting on the floor, her back against the modern angular couch, and she was bleeding all over that beautiful wood. I gasped and everyone in the room turned to look at me.

I probably hadn't been supposed to do that. Too late.

Julie had Yasmina propped up against her and, pressing something into her shoulder, and there was blood on her hands. "Where is he?" Ali asked her.

"I don't know," Julie said. "I didn't see him. I came in right after the shooting." She jerked her head to her left and I could see feet protruding from behind a chair. Ali moved quickly over to it and made a small noise that sounded piteous. It had to be one of his guys. I shivered. "Did you call for an ambulance?" I asked Julie. I could at least do something useful if she hadn't. Yasmina didn't look conscious.

"I've called for everything we've got," she said. She looked pale; but Yasmina looked blue. I wondered if she were still alive.

Ali came back. "Got both of them," he said, his voice savage, then asked Julie, "How long ago?"

"Three minutes," she said. I guessed that police must be trained to notice the time whenever anything untoward happened; and this was about as untoward as it got. "Where—" I started asking Ali, when there was another huge crack, only it wasn't thunder, and Ali was on top of me, his gun magically in his hand again. "Stay down," he said, fiercely, then moved away. Another explosion, and one of the huge plate-glass windows spectacularly shattered, the wind and rain immediately blowing in.

I stayed where I was, even when the lights went out.

"Avery!" Julie shouted. "This isn't going to end well. Come out and give yourself up!"

There was another shot—my brain had finally identified the explosions as gunshot—and Ali cursed and I felt rather than saw him move, fast, over to my right. Ever the heroine, I stayed huddled where I was. There was a siren coming closer; we could barely hear it over the sound of the wind. "Avery!" yelled Ali. "Don't make it worse for yourself!"

Still no response. Yasmina moaned; I'd wondered if she were dead. "We have to do something before they get here," said Julie to no one in particular. "I don't want them walking into a live scene."

I personally wasn't thrilled to be a part of the live scene, myself. I scooted farther back against the wall and immediately fell over something big and squishy. I gasped and pulled myself away from it and in the next lightning flash peered at it just as another bullet found another window and the storm roared in anew. "Ali," I yelled.

"What?" His voice seemed far away.

I started to talk again and found my throat closing. *You are so not going to throw up.* I pulled myself up on my feet. "We have a problem!" I finally managed to shout, the wind grabbing my voice and tossing it around the room so that it echoed back at me.

"*What?*" he yelled again.

"Anthony Avery's over here!" I yelled. "I think he's dead! It's not him shooting!"

And then that cologne, that expensive men's cologne, enveloped me as Jason said, "That's right, honey. It's me."

23

I fainted.

How incredibly humiliating is that? I swear I've never fainted in my whole life, not ever. But I chose my moment well; if Jason had planned to grab me and use me as a shield, then I took care of that plan right away: I'm not fat but as a dead weight I was too much for him to handle.

That's what Ali said later, anyway. When Jason was in a cell at the Provincetown police station waiting for the sheriff to pick him up, and Yasmina had been transported to Cape Cod Hospital up in Hyannis, and I was curled up in the living room of Barry's suite at the inn, Glenn giving me French hot chocolate and me feeling completely foolish and at the same time completely delighted to still be breathing.

What happened after I passed out was that Ali saw me go down and yelled for Jason's attention and Julie grabbed him and that was the end of that. They seemed to think it was a simple and obvious manoeuver. For them, perhaps, it was. It certainly sounded smooth enough when they recounted it. "He killed Barry?" I asked, still sounding stupid. "He couldn't have." I'd liked Jason. I'd always liked Jason.

Glenn sat next to me and put my hands around the cup. "Drink some of that," he said, encouragingly.

"I don't understand," I said, again.

I didn't know how long I'd been out. I was wearing a fluffy robe from the inn's spa. Ali's hair was completely dry. Had I been in a *coma*?

"Jason killed Barry," said Ali. "This whole trafficking thing—well, I don't have any doubt that Anthony Avery was going to act, sooner rather than later, but Jason accelerated his plan. He needed a fall guy and Avery showed up at just the right time. Jason told him that Yasmina knew as much about the trafficking as Barry did. Jason wanted everyone up there so that he could kill Avery—after making sure that Avery would get blamed for the rest. And yeah, Jason had already killed Barry. I'm sorry, Sydney."

"I'm sorry, too," I echoed. I was getting that distinctly Alice-Through-The-Looking-Glass feeling again. "Why?"

Glenn prodded me and I obediently took a swallow of the exquisite hot chocolate. Outside, it was nighttime. The storm had passed. "It was about money, just on a lesser scale," said Ali.

"On a lesser scale than what?"

"Jason's been embezzling from Race Point for more than a year," Glenn said. "Serious money, that's why I spotted it right away. Don't know why Mike hadn't." His pause didn't bode well for Mike. "Barry found out and fired Jason. That was the night of the Hawaiian party, and Barry gave Jason a week to stay and pretend that leaving was Jason's idea." He swallowed. "He was too good, in the end."

"But that wasn't good enough for Jason," I said. I could see where this was going.

Ali said, "He was living beyond his means already, buying a condo, planning a vacation in Italy." *Right*, I thought, remembering grabbing Jason's phone from him and seeing the

Zillow listings. *I should have wondered why he was looking at real estate.*

Glenn was watching me. "There's nothing you could have done," he said, gently.

"Where did he get the gun? When did he learn to shoot?" That didn't sound much like the Jason I'd known. But none of this did.

Ali said, "Julie's tracking that down. We think he probably didn't plan to kill so many people, but when he found out we were looking at Anthony Avery, it was his opportunity to throw one tremendous red herring into the mix and cover his own tracks. That was why he sent you that text last night, by the way. He knew you wouldn't be able to resist following up. And Avery would be dead and get blamed for everything."

"He was a quick study," I said bitterly; I hadn't been much of a quick study myself. One of my friends killing another. It was so Shakespearean. Or Gothic. Or something.

"He was smart, and pretty good at everything he did," said Ali. He seemed to know more about Jason than I had. "What about Yasmina?" I asked.

"She'll need some physical therapy, but she'll be fine."

"Is Julie moving into the Gropius house?" He smiled. "Not yet."

"It's going to be expensive to repair," I said. "All that glass, all that water damage…" *And all those memories from today*, I added silently.

Glenn cleared his throat. "I'm grateful to both of you," he said awkwardly. "Barry would have been disappointed to know that Jason could do something like this, but I know he'd have been pleased to know there were people who risked their lives like this."

It was a nice little speech. I peered at him over the rim of my mug. "What're you going to do now?"

"I'm selling the bar in Key West," he said. "The Race Point Inn needs a fulltime owner, and it looks like that's me." He caught Ali's expression, and added, "Um—without the green-card weddings, of course." He looked back at me. "And I'm hoping that you'll stay on as wedding coordinator, Sydney."

I nodded. I couldn't imagine being anywhere else. Provincetown does get into your blood. I looked at Ali, and he grinned. "Don't look so pleased with yourself," I said to him.

"All's well that ends well," he said.

"I guess I need to get used to the Shakespeare quotations," I said, and he smiled even more broadly. "I guess you do," he said.

Breathe, Riley. Just breathe.

Acknowledgments

Thanks to Meredith Kurkjian Lobur for giving me insights into police procedure on the Cape; to Cary Cahill for taking me on a tour of the Gropius house (a seriously amazing place); and to Assaf Levavy for being a faithful beta reader.

And thank also to Arthur Mahoney of Homeport Press for being one of the nicest publishers *ever*.

Did You Enjoy This Book?

If you did…

Please share your opinion on Goodreads, Amazon, BN.com, and Powell's.

Visit my Amazon page and read some of my other books.

Give the book a boost on by telling people about it on Facebook and Twitter.

Subscribe to The Novelist's Notebook at www.JeannetteDeBeauvoir.com (scroll to bottom of page) for book reviews, short stories, quizzes, free stuff, previews of upcoming work, and more.

Ask your local bookseller to stock *Death of a Bear*.

Make it your choice for your next book club meeting. (I'll even join you by Skype if you'd like me to!)

Email me at JeannettedeBeauvoir @ gmail.com and tell me so!

And watch for the next in the P'town Theme Week series, *Murder at Fantasia Fair*, coming in October 2017 from Homeport Press!

Made in the USA
Lexington, KY
08 April 2018